P9-DNU-463

RECEIVED
OCT 22 2009
By

THROUGH THE FIRE

"Why are you here, Quinn?" Rae asked. Her eyes dragged over his face, memorizing the contours, the sweep of his brows, the depth of his dark eyes, the perfect symmetry of his lips, the smooth chocolate of his skin. She wanted to touch him, taste him, have him hold her again, and her hold him back. She wanted to feel him inside of her, if only for a moment, just long enough to remember what it felt like to be a woman. She hadn't wanted that with anyone for so long, couldn't bear the thought of a man other than her husband touching her. But Sterling was gone and she was still here. She was still alone, still afraid—even now when the man who'd made her blood heat again was mere inches away.

"I'm not sure why I came, Rae," Quinn finally answered. "All I know is that I couldn't stop thinkin' about you all night. I woke up this morning and you were here." He tapped his temple. "Right there in my head, messin' with my mind."

THROUGH THE FIRE

Donna Hill

BET Publications, LLC

ARABESQUE BOOKS are published by

BET Publications, LLC
c/o BET BOOKS
One BET Plaza
1900 W Place NE
Washington, D.C. 20018-1211

ISBN 0-7394-1788-6

Printed in the United States of America

Chapter One

Quinten Parker rolled over in bed, feeling the cool, empty space beside him. Each day for the past three years he'd hoped that he'd awake and the longing, the emptiness would be over—Nikita would be beside him, curled along the length of his body.

He released a sigh, adjusted his eyes to the light of a new day. Nothing had changed. The heaviness still hung in his heart and in his loins—a sensation that hadn't been quenched or filled by anything or anyone.

In the distance he heard his landlady, Mrs. Finch, moving around downstairs. A faint smile touched his lips. Some of the familiar things were still good. Yet, his friends Nick and Parris had repeatedly tried to convince him to move away from the place that he and Nikita had shared as man and wife. "You need to move on, start over," they'd insisted. "Too many memories." But the memories were all he had left. The things that kept him company when the loneliness became too much to handle.

"Daddy. . . I'm hungry," came a tiny sleep-filled voice.

Quinn's chest filled with an almost unspeakable joy as he was momentarily taken aback at seeing the tiny version of himself staring boldly back at him. He sat up in the bed, the white sheet slipping to his waist, unveiling his bare chest.

"What would you like today, buddy?"

"Pancakes!" Jamel said with a wide grin, revealing a missing front tooth.

Quinn chuckled and threw his long legs over the side of the bed. The past four weeks had been pure magic—the first big block of time he'd spent with his son. He'd tried to squeeze six years into those four weeks. Sure, he'd been to San Francisco to visit several times during the year, but he'd never had this much time, all at once, one-on-one. It was an experience he wouldn't soon forget.

He'd learned things about himself during their time together. He learned that he was a good teacher as he helped his son figure out how to connect all the game wires to the television. He learned that he was capable of being a nurturer when he held his son at night and read to him, or bandaged a wounded knee. He learned that he still had the capacity to feel, to want to care, to want to do something for someone else, to give something of himself to another human being. He hadn't thought Maxine would agree to his request to have Jamel spend part of the summer with him. She'd surprised him when she agreed and told him "it was time." For that, he would always be grateful.

Quinn stood and came around the foot of the bed, swooping Jamel up from the floor and tucking him beneath his arm to delighted giggles and squirming.

"Pancakes, huh?" He pushed a finger into Jamel's side and wiggled it, eliciting more laughter. It was music to his ears, lyrical and perfect like the chords he'd once played on the piano. But it was about to end and his life would return to what he'd grown accustomed to—trying to make it one day at a time.

Quinn spoke in quiet, but decisive tones to the stewardess who'd promised to look after Jamel during the six-hour flight back to the coast.

"Please don't worry, Mr. Parker," she insisted, placing a comforting hand on Quinn's hard bicep. "He'll be fine."

Quinn looked down at his son, who held his hand in a viselike grip, but otherwise appeared excited about his journey. "This nice lady . . ." He glanced at the name tag on her navy blue lapel. ". . . Ms. Traynor is going to take care of you on the plane, J. If you need anything, you ask her. Okay?"

Jamel nodded, his dark eyes taking in the sights around him. He stuck a lollipop in his mouth and talked around it. "I'm a big boy, Daddy," he said with all the assurance of his six years.

Daddy. His heart fluttered for a moment as the corner of his rich mouth quirked upward into a half smile. "That you are, little man." He rustled his tight curls.

"I'd better get him settled on board," the stewardess said gently.

Quinn stooped down to Jamel's eye level, bracing his thin shoulders. "I had a great time, little man."

"Me too."

"Mommy will be there to meet you when you get off the plane."

Jamel nodded and sucked a bit harder on his lollipop.

"I'll call you tonight." Quinn tugged in a breath and drew Jamel's small frame close to his body. He hugged him tight, wanting to hold on to those last moments forever—needing Jamel to know just how much he was loved, how much he mattered, the difference that his presence had made in his life—if only momentarily. "I love you, son," he whispered, hearing the hitch in his voice.

"I love you too, Daddy."

Quinn gave Jamel one last squeeze and quickly stood before he broke down; that was something Jamel didn't need to see.

The stewardess extended her hand to Jamel and led him down the boarding entrance. She looked over her shoulder and mouthed, "He'll be fine."

Quinn pressed his lips together, swallowing over the knot in his throat as he stood framed in the wide window watching the plane take off and disappear into the cloudless summer morning. He tugged in a breath. As sad as he felt after separating from his son once again, this time it was with a sense of hope, of possibility. A feeling he'd forgotten how to experience. Hope, that there was a possibility for a life, a real life, though different from the one he'd once imagined.

"Your son needs you, Quinten," Mrs. Finch had counseled, during Jamel's four-week stay. "But the boy needs more than the shell of the man you've become. Let *her* go, son,'' she'd whispered, clasping his large hand in her thin, frail ones.

Quinn's insides contracted and his chest became full as they did any time the thought of Nikita was evoked, her name was mentioned or even alluded to. He heaved in a breath. When would it ever end? When?

He turned away from the window, head bowed, and started off toward the exit. The truth was, he mused as he caught glimpses of happy, hand-holding couples and laughing families, he didn't like who he'd become these last three years. Didn't like how he moved through his day like a shadow, there but untouchable. He hadn't written a piece of music since Nikita's death, hadn't played in the band, hadn't written a word for his long overdue second novel. All he'd done was try to find a way to open his eyes each morning and hope that he could get through the pain of the day until he could close them again.

He turned on the engine in his Navigator and eased out into the airport traffic. He wanted his life back—*a* life back, filled with that joy he'd once known. But he was terrified. Terrified of how that pain would feel if he ever dared to love and lose again.

Chapter Two

When Quinn returned to the house, Mrs. Finch was, as usual, out front sweeping the yard. He shook his head in amusement as he alighted from the van and headed toward the wrought-iron gate. Mrs. Finch was no more sweeping the walkway than he was an astronaut. Her only purpose for that raggedy broom was to give her some semblance of legitimacy as she eagle-eyed the comings and goings of her neighbors. An almost religious activity she'd indulged in for as long as he'd known her.

"You missed a spot, Mrs. Finch," Quinn wryly commented, fighting down a grin.

Mrs. Finch squeezed her eyes into what she believed to be a formidable stare and pointed a slender finger at the towering form in front of her.

"Don't you sass me, Quinten Parker."

"Yes, ma'am," he mumbled, his dark eyes twinkling. To this day, she was still the only person he allowed to call him Quinten.

She leaned on her broom. "So . . . how was it?"

Quinn's expression darkened. He looked away for a moment, then back at her. He shrugged. "Awright. Not bad."

She looked him over, registering the hollowness in his eyes that had abated during Jamel's visit, but had taken up residence once again.

"Hmmm," she murmured, reaching out to pat his shoulder. "Life is hard, son. But we get through it. Think of this as a new start instead of an ending."

Quinn looked at his surrogate mother skeptically.

"I know you don't see it now. But you will. If you give yourself a chance."

Just as Quinn opened his mouth to object, Mrs. Finch cut him off. "I need you to go to the supermarket and pick up a few things for me and stop at the vegetable stand, too." She reached into the pocket of her pink-and-white checkered shift and pulled out a piece of paper and a roll of one-dollar bills. "Here's the list and the money. If it's not enough, you add the rest." She waved her hand dismissively. "I'll give it back to you . . . later."

Quinn peered at her from beneath his thick lashes, his brows raised. He'd been running errands for Mrs. Finch for six years. She had yet to give him enough money to purchase anything. If it was a pack of gum for a quarter, she would assuredly give him a dime. If he added up all the money she owed to him he'd be a very wealthy man. But he loved her.

"And don't take too long," she warned. "I want to get my supper started early. Smothered chicken," she singsonged to his retreating form, knowing it was one of his favorites.

He shook his head and chuckled. She always knew how to get to him.

Quinn sauntered into the supermarket, the blast of cold air smacking him, raising the chill bumps on his bare arms. He slipped his dark glasses off his nose and slid them into the top pocket of his black sleeveless T-shirt. Grabbing a noisy shopping cart he headed toward the frozen food aisle. He opened one of the freezer doors and pulled out a can of Coke. He popped the top and thought immediately of Nikita. It was her favorite drink—with lemon. After being with her those few short years, he'd found himself addicted to it as well. So many things, he thought, so much of who she was had become a part of him. No one could understand that kind of love, why it was so hard for him to let go and move on with his life. Sometimes it seemed as if the very air he breathed held her scent.

"Can't be that bad," a throaty voice from his right commented, the words lilting like the verse to a song.

Quinn turned his eyes in the direction of the melody. The face was familiar, but he couldn't quite place it. " 'Scuse me?"

"I said, it can't be that bad." Her steady gaze appraised him, the first time she'd actually seen him up close. He was even more dangerously handsome in person.

He cut his eyes back to the freezer and shut the door. "Maybe it is," he returned in a monotone. He adjusted his body to face her. She was tall, he subconsciously registered, full and firm. Not bad. Not interested.

"If you believe it, then you will make it be."

Quinn laughed in his throat. "So what are you . . . some kinda fortune-teller or something?" He lightly ran his tongue across his lips.

She smiled and all of a sudden, something inside him moved as if the darkness had been pushed aside with a beam of bright light. The sensation was so immediate, so powerful it was physical. He swallowed over the sudden dryness in his throat stunned by the inexplicable sexual arousal that was making itself boldly evident against the confines of his jeans. Her smile wrapped itself around him like loving arms, stroking him so tenderly that he felt his heart beat out of time. He needed to get away from her, away from whatever it was she was doing to him—with a simple smile.

"You're Quinten Parker, aren't you? I've seen your picture in the back of your book and on your CD cover. You haven't done anything in a while. You're missed."

"Fan?"

"Ego stoking?" she countered.

Slowly, Quinn began to relax, allowing himself to get reacquainted with the bob and weave of the mating game, the preliminary chat. "You're on point, huh?"

"I've spent too much time in my life biting my tongue and being diplomatic." A momentary shadow passed across her warm brown eyes. "It cost me."

"Sorry to hear that."

She shrugged. "We all have to move on."

Quinn stared at her for a moment, that all too familiar refrain settling like a weight in his belly. "What if you can't?"

"Then we stay in that same place, unchanged and hurting." Her unwavering stare held him in place. "And we lose the essence of what life is all about—evolution and change."

The corner of his mouth quirked upward. "Sounds like you've thought about it a lot."

She glanced away, focusing on the contents of her cart. "I've had time," she stated simply. She took a breath, then suddenly brightened. "You like poetry?"

Quinn shrugged. "Some."

She pulled a flyer out of her purse. "Come down to Encore tonight. You might enjoy yourself." She handed him the flyer and began to move away. "Nice to meet you, Quinten Parker."

Quinn watched her walk away, studying the sensuous sway of her hips, the way her hair in curly twists caressed her face, until she turned down another aisle and was gone. He glanced at the flyer in his hand: *Rae Lindsay—Appearing Tonight at Encore.* Rae Lindsay? He folded the flyer and shoved it into the back pocket of his jeans, intent on dismissing the entire episode. The name sounded familiar, but he couldn't place it, though he felt he should. He shrugged. Didn't matter anyhow. The last place he wanted to spend his Saturday night was sitting up in some club somewhere—too many memories. That's where he'd met Nikita, that's where he'd returned to finally commit himself to her. Naw, Encore was out.

But the lovely woman, with the piercing eyes and melodic voice, who spoke poignant truths, had wiggled her way beneath his armor, and there she remained.

* * *

Quinn lay sprawled across his bed, the encroaching evening and the hum of the air conditioner his only company. Maxine had called earlier to let him know that Jamel had arrived safely, and they chatted briefly about his trip and how happy he seemed. That made Quinn feel good, knowing that Jamel's visit didn't have any ill effects.

"How's Taylor?" Quinn asked, wanting and not wanting to know. He could hear the smile in her voice when she talked about her husband.

"He's wonderful. His business is doing great, and he's been talking about opening another office."

"Sounds good, Max. Glad to hear it."

They were quiet for a moment.

"How about you, Q? How are you doing?"

"Hey, can't complain. Taking it light, ya know."

"Getting out any—meet anyone?"

"No to both."

"Why, Q? You can't live in a vacuum forever. Nikita wouldn't have—"

"Don't, Max. Awright? Leave it alone." His jaw clenched.

"If we've ever been anything to each other, Q, it's been honest. And you know good and damn well you've never been able to tell me what to do."

He shut his eyes, knowing how right she was. "Yeah, yeah."

"I know you don't want to hear it, but I'm gonna say it anyway: Nikita is gone, Q. She's not coming back, not even if you sit and grieve from now till the end of time. But you are here. You have a life, a career, a future—a son. It's up to you to decide what you're going to do about them. I never knew you to half-step about anything, Q, to crawl in a corner and pull the sheet up over your head. But that's what you've been doing these three years. And you're not the man I once knew . . . once loved. And definitely not the kind of man you want to be for your son. The choice is yours, babe. I gotta go get J ready for bed and everything. Call him during the week. Okay?"

"Yeah," he mumbled. "I will."

"Take care, Q."

"Yeah . . . and, Max . . ."

"Yes?"

"Thanks."

"Later, Q."

Quinn thought about that conversation now, and the countless others that were so similar. He knew they were right, but it just seemed that he'd lost his will, his drive, and he didn't know what to do to get it back. He turned on his side and spotted the flyer on his night table. Sitting up, he smoothed out the wrinkled edges against the firmness of the tabletop and reread the invitation. A picture of the woman in the supermarket took shape in his head, and he wondered if *she* was Rae Lindsay. Something told him she was.

Getting up, he walked out of the bedroom and went downstairs into the living room straight for his collection of CDs. Sifting through them, he flipped each one to the back, looking for the names of contributors. Out of the first dozen he'd scanned, five had Rae Lindsay's name clearly noted as songwriter. Songs that he'd listened to and enjoyed, both as a means of entertainment and with a musician's ear.

Imagine that. You really couldn't judge a book by its cover. Rae Lindsay; a sister with not only a strong presence but with something profound and creative underneath. As a musician, he knew how difficult it was to bring together all of the various elements that make up a good song, that fascinating mix of words and music that can bring tears to a listener's eyes, lift someone's spirits, or recall memories of times long gone. For this reason alone, she was not a woman he could easily dismiss.

And so he found himself seated at a front row table at Encore, the first time he'd stepped inside a nightclub in three years. When he arrived at the place, there were two young brothers, one on an upright bass and another on flute, backing a tall, dark-skinned woman reading poetry. Dressed in casual garb, she adjusted the thin straps of her mink brown silk top, revealing the strong lines of her arms, the subtle tones blending seamlessly with her flesh, making them one. The stage lighting in the club cast light and dark shadows across the figure seated regally on the stool, giving the scene the illusion of a dream. Maybe it was intentional, Quinn thought, as he found himself closing his eyes, swept into the musical rhythm of the words, hypnotized from the play of light, and the lush voice. Much of what the woman read sounded like a cross between the fiery poetry of Sonia Sanchez revved up on hip-hop and the bold verse of Nikki Giovanni updated for a new generation. He found the lilting sound of the flute tantalizing and subtly seductive. Poetically, she weaved her words between the notes, adding accents and flavor to each of her choruses, playing her audience's energy with all the skill of a minister working a revival. By the end of her segment, the entire house was on its feet, cheering her. Everyone except Quinn.

He was beyond applause. What he'd experienced in her magical rendering of words tapped into a part of him that had long been dormant—the melody of him—the part he'd buried, sworn was dead. It wasn't. His heart thudded in time to the beat of hands. The houselights came up and Rae Lindsay took her bow.

Chapter Three

Rae moved fluidly from the stage, still wrapped in the prose that had flowed from her soul. When she'd sat in the window seat of her bedroom watching the sun peek between the two trees in her yard, it was then that it came to her, the magic memory of a love that would never die. She wanted to find a way to convey that kind of passion, the depth that comes from finally realizing what one once had. Sterling had offered it and Akia was born of it—foolishly she took it for granted and lost. She wanted to find that kind of love again, but didn't know if she ever would.

"Impressive."

Rae focused on the figure in front of her, smiling faintly, letting go of the memories. "Thank you." Her heart beat just a bit faster, as a slow but steady warmth moved through her body.

Their gazes held each other in that tenuous moment of uncertainty. That instant when unconscious decisions are made and lives are irrevocably changed.

Quinn shifted his stance, and Rae felt all the air, the energy around her vibrate. She swallowed, momentarily unsure of herself and of what was happening to her. She hadn't been able to get him out of her head all day. When she least expected it she would suddenly see him standing in front of her, dark and erotically lethal, the shuddering virility of him barely contained beneath the cool control of his demeanor. Quinten Parker was all male. The kind of male good girls were taught to stay away from. The kind of male who could steal your heart with a look, capture your soul with a smile, and claim your body with a simple touch.

"Can I buy you a drink?" he asked, not wanting her to leave just yet.

"Yes," she answered before she even realized the word was out of her mouth. And when he placed his hand lightly along the soft hollow of her spine, she knew Quinten Parker was more than she'd bargained for.

Quinn stirred the squares of ice in his glass of Jack Daniels, seemingly intent on the slow, almost hypnotic way the amber liquid drifted in and out of the cubes' dips and curves.

Rae watched his hands, the long, sinewy piano fingers that had mesmerized her with their skills. For an instant she wondered how talented they really were when bare flesh was offered for exploration.

Her nipples suddenly hardened at the image, and she shifted in her seat. The quiet intensity of him was maddening.

"I didn't think you'd come," she finally said, unable to handle the silence a moment longer.

Quinn glanced up from beneath his lashes. "Wasn't in my plans." He took a sip of his drink.

"Then why did you?"

He shrugged slightly and ran his tongue along his lips before answering. "A man can have a change of heart, can't he?" He stared directly at her, a dark challenge in his eyes, the shadow of a smile on his lips.

She wasn't going to let him rattle her, she silently vowed. *He's just a man.* Rae straightened in her chair, took a sip of her screwdriver, then leaned forward. "Why'd you stop playing?" It wasn't the first time she'd seen the cool facade momentarily melt away. But he recovered quickly.

"Same reason I came here tonight. Change of heart," he added, his last comment losing some of its bite.

"Because of your wife?"

His eyes snapped in her direction. He signaled for the waitress without taking his eyes off Rae. "Another one," he said without looking up when the waitress appeared. "And one for the lady." Finally he looked away. "Not something I care to talk about, ya know."

"Your playing . . . or your wife?"

"Are you always so damned direct?"

She didn't miss the sudden sparkle in his eyes. "Whenever I can be. Like I said to you earlier, I've spent too much time dodging the facts, holding things in, not dealing with the issues. I'm working on not being that woman anymore."

Quinn was quiet for a moment, contemplative. What had changed her? he wondered, transforming her into this bold, challenging woman who spoke the words of the elders—wise, all-seeing, thought-provoking? Yet for all her exterior control he sensed something beneath the surface. He'd seen the look in her eyes before—seen it in his own. He'd heard the soul-wrenching poetic verse before. He too had spoken the words. Those were the things that attracted him to her, not her in-your-face approach, but what lay beneath the words, the background vocals that held the song in place, and played over and again in your mind.

"What changed you?" Quinn asked quietly.

Rae's lips pinched for a moment, as something old, something gone passed across her eyes. "Loss," she said simply.

Their gazes held each other and understanding beyond mere words formed between them and joined hands.

"Husband?"

Ray nodded stiffly. "And my . . . daughter. She was five."

"How long?"

"Three years."

Quinn felt a tightness in his chest. *Nikita.* He took a long swallow of his drink, then clasped the glass in both hands, staring down at the melting ice, a time that was forever gone. "Sometimes I wake up and think it's all a bad dream," he confessed quietly.

"I know." Rae laughed sadly. "So do I. But it isn't." She pulled in a breath, then let it out slowly. "But my work gets me through it. I don't know what I'd do otherwise." She glanced across the flickering flame cupped in the glass goblet that separated them. "I read about your wife in the papers. I'm sorry," she said sincerely. "It's so ironic that we should lose the ones we loved at virtually the same time." She paused for a moment, framing her words. "At the time it was as if we—you and I—were connected. I know this sounds crazy, but . . . I seemed to know how you were feeling, what you were going through, because it was happening to me as well. I was in the same place. I wanted to write to you . . . and tell you, but I thought it would be an intrusion. And I knew how empty 'I'm so sorry' sounded to *my* ears."

Her confession, her willingness to allow him to enter that private space in her soul seemed to release him somehow. Release him in a way that nothing or no one had really been able to do before. A part of him realized that she would understand because she'd been there, too.

"Things were so strange back then, disconnected. It was as if I were walking in a haze all the time. I couldn't think, couldn't sleep. Felt like the world was moving but I was standing still, ya know." He took a swallow of his drink. "I'd wake up sometimes sure that it was all a bad dream." He heaved in a breath. "You're right . . . about the 'I'm so sorry.' It didn't help. Still doesn't."

"What does?" Rae asked, wanting to know if he'd found a way to start living again, some key that she'd missed.

"I haven't figured that out yet." He almost smiled.

"You will. When you give yourself a chance, open yourself up to possibility. At least that's what everyone tells me." She chuckled half-heartedly not quite believing it herself.

The old refrain played again. He didn't want to go there. He'd heard it from every person he came into contact with. They all believed they knew what was best for him, what would make his life worth living again. They said all the right things. They tried. But the truth was they had no idea what he needed, how he felt. He glanced at Rae. He believed that she did. He wasn't sure why, he just did. "Yeah," he finally mumbled. "You have another set, or what?"

"No. I'm finished for tonight."

"Any plans?"

"Nothing special. What about you?"

"I figured . . . maybe we could get to know each other better. I mean, if it's cool with you." He gazed at her pointedly, a shadow of a smile playing around his mouth.

Rae angled her head to the right and arched her brow. "How do you know I don't have a man waiting in the wings?"

Quinn leaned back in the chair. "Hey, if you do it's not a problem. I know my way home. But you don't seem to be the kind of woman who would sit around sharing drinks with a man—tryin' to get to know him—if you had one waiting." He cocked his head to the side, mirroring her pose, and looked at her lazily.

At that moment he reminded her of a long, sleek

panther chilling on a flat rock high above his prey, coolly surveying all below, ready to pounce on the unsuspecting. She couldn't let him get that chance. It was clear what he wanted, and she wasn't sure if she was ready, didn't think she could handle what might happen between them. At least not now. Not yet, maybe never.

"It's getting late," Rae finally said, needing an escape. She took her purse from the table and stood. "Thanks . . . for the drinks . . . and the conversation." She stuck out her hand.

Slowly Quinn reached for it, taking her hand completely in his. The warmth and surprising softness of it flowed through his limbs, to his head, and the heat rushed straight to the throb that pulsed between his thighs the instant he touched her. And at the same time he felt strangely connected to this woman as if some missing link had finally been discovered and slipped into place. But that couldn't be, because that's not what he wanted from her. His jaw clenched. Yeah, it was best that she did leave.

She was wet. A simple touch from this man and she was as wet as if she'd participated in a naughty game of foreplay. This she didn't need. Not when she was finally putting her life back in order, piecing together the tattered fragments of her emotions. She wasn't ready for a man like Quinten Parker.

"I—I'd better go," she mumbled, hearing her words flutter like flapping wings.

Quinten stood, too, as if pulled by some invisible thread. "I'll walk you to your car."

"I didn't drive. I only live a few blocks away."

"Then I'll walk you home." *What am I doing?*

"I—"

"You shouldn't be walkin' the street alone. It's almost two."

Rae pulled in a breath, hoping to slow down the racing of her heart. "All right," she mumbled.

As always, even at that hour of the morning, the streets of the city, specifically the West Village, were still peppered with people of every ilk. Neon lights from the rows of bars cast a rainbow of color along the avenue. Laughter mixed with music, drifted around them, the waning warmth of the summer night keeping perfect time.

Rae and Quinn walked in silence along West Fourth Street. Each acutely aware of the other, but wary of breaking the tenuous silence for all that it would stir up between them.

She's nothing like Nikita, Quinn mused, taking furtive, sidelong glances at Rae. She was tall, slender, and self-contained. And although she had an aggressive manner, there was a cautiousness about her. Her complexion reminded him of brandy—tempting and warm through and through. She was pretty in a laid-back sense, not cover-model pretty like Nikita, but a comfortable beauty that gets better with age. He could see the strong strains of the ancestors in the cut of her cheekbones, the curve of her full lips, the flair of her nose. Yeah, Rae Lindsay was easy on the eye, and talented to boot—an intoxicating combination. It had been a long time since he'd thought of a woman for any more than her ability to quench the physical fire that constantly smoldered within him. But none had. None had been able to fill the longing, to stamp down the embers. What he'd been seeking was something none of them had been able to give—a sense of being home again, being able to feel again. Too much of him had gone dead inside. He knew he shouldn't compare every woman he met with Nikita. It wasn't fair. No one would ever be able to take her place—or at least replace the image he'd created of her. Over time the things that had once driven him mad about her were now miraculously endearing; what they'd fought over was no longer important; the way she'd wanted to rearrange his life was now cute. In his mind Nikita had evolved into the personification of perfection. It was so much easier to remember her that way. And he had yet to meet anyone able to shatter the image he'd constructed. Sometimes he thought that maybe it was better that way.

He came up short, his thoughts scattering, when Rae stopped in front of a neatly kept redbrick building.

"This is where I get off," she said, the first words spoken since they'd left the club. "Thanks for the company." She turned and looked up into his eyes. "And for coming down tonight."

"It was cool—worth it." He shoved his hands into the pockets of his lightweight leather jacket, more to keep from touching her than from trying to create an image.

"Well . . . I'd better go." She wanted to touch him, gently brush away the lock that caressed his cheek. But she dared not.

Quinn glanced up at the darkened windows, wondering which one was hers. "When will you be performing again?" He wanted to keep her there just a moment longer—just to hold on to this feeling a little longer. *Feeling.* His stomach tightened.

"I'm not sure. I need to work on some songs and I've gotten behind my deadline."

"You, uh, work from home or at a studio?"

"Both." She smiled. "It depends on everyone's schedule. Actually, studio time is scheduled for next Wednesday. Maybe . . . you'd like to sit in." *Oh, Lord, what am I doing?*

He hadn't set foot in a studio in nearly three years. His own CD was long overdue. He just hadn't been able to bring himself to—"What time Wednesday?" he asked before he realized the question had crossed his lips and he couldn't take it back.

"Nine in the morning. We'll be at it all day."

He shrugged. "Cool. Maybe I'll check you out."

Rae dug in her purse for her wallet and pulled out a business card. "Here's the address," she said, handing him the gold-leafed, embossed card.

Quinn reached for it. Their fingertips brushed and they were both jolted by the contact.

For a moment neither of them moved, neither dared to speak until the current had run its course.

"Thanks," Quinn uttered, wanting to kiss her instead of saying good-bye.

"So, uh, maybe I'll see you Wednesday." Rae clasped the straps of her shoulder bag with both hands.

"Yeah. Maybe." Quinn jutted his chin toward the steps of Rae's building. "You oughta go on in."

Rae released a nervous puff of air, smiling inanely before taking two steps back, then starting up the steps. "Good night," she tossed over her shoulder, opened the door, and stepped inside, shutting it behind her.

Quinn stood there for a minute until he saw lights in the third-floor window slide through the slats of the blinds. He made a note to himself, then headed back to the club to retrieve his Jeep.

Rae watched his departure from the darkened window of her bedroom and knew with certainty that Quinten Parker might be walking away, but he would be back. She didn't know how she knew it, she just did.

Chapter Four

Quinn moved slowly through his apartment, the warmth of a new day bouncing off the plants in the window.

The spacious rooms seemed more empty than usual today, now that Jamel was back in San Francisco with his mother. He'd grown accustomed to Jamel's early morning wake-up call of "Daddy, I'm hungry." He smiled, pulling sheets off the bed for the laundry, while promising himself that he would call his son later in the day.

He shoved the sheets, then damp towels in a laundry bag and set it by the door. It was good having someone in your life, he grudgingly admitted, hauling the bag down the stairs and out to his Jeep, hoping to slide under Mrs. Finch's radar before she snagged him for some errand or another. He turned the key and the soothing hum of the engine vibrated beneath him.

He missed having someone to look out for, care about, someone he could come home to and share his day with. He'd always been a loner, content to do his thing by himself. Until he'd met Nikita. She'd changed all that for him. And after he'd lost her, he knew without a doubt that he'd never have those feelings again, those needs again. But having his son with him had relit the fire that had been doused by pain and disillusionment, and meeting Rae Lindsay had been like tossing kindling on the smoldering flames. But was he truly ready to walk through the fire to the promise of possibility on the other side? He was no longer sure if he knew how.

Rae sat on the piano bench, her nimble fingers tinkering with the keys. A new arrangement of notes for a song had haunted her throughout the night. Several times she'd gotten out of bed and found her way to the baby grand that sat like a Buddha in the center of her living room. The melody would come to her in bursts, then fade, and she would stumble back to bed only to be magnetically drawn back moments later.

It was always this way with her—this creative thing that she could not control. Sometimes it would creep up on her like a thief stealing all conscious thought, only leaving behind the seed of challenge. *Catch me. Capture me. Expose me for all the world to see and hear.* And she would be compelled to create. Compelled to play. Twist the standard notes into something never before heard. Write the words that would echo in hearts and minds for always.

She was in that space now—the zone, where nothing else mattered beyond this thing as necessary to her life as breathing. And between each note, each turn of phrase, she remembered her evening with Quinn Parker, and knew it was he who was the catalyst for this roller-coaster ride she was on.

Rae rose stiffly from the bench and arched her back to loosen the kinks that gripped her spine. Her gaze drifted toward the window. The world moved in a steady hum on the other side of the glass—removed from her—the way she always felt—disconnected. Except yesterday, for the first time in longer than she could remember.

She'd buried herself so deeply in her work these past three years, she didn't allow herself time to think, to feel, to experience life around her. She'd been too afraid. So she surrounded herself with her music, musicians, friends, anything to keep the memories at bay, her guilt under wraps. Her music, her lyrics became the cocoon that protected her. But somehow meeting Quinn had weakened the protective covering, leaving her tender insides exposed and vulnerable. She wasn't sure how he was able to accomplish what so many had tried and failed to do. But he had.

Rae wrapped her arms tightly around her waist, as if the action could somehow contain the brewing emotions, the awakening of sensations that bubbled with life within her.

His eyes—dark, soulful, full of seeing too much. His mouth—rich, sculpted, and tender. His voice—like the roll of waves rushing to the shore, carrying a unique rhythm with each ebb and flow. She felt him. Something she'd been unable to do for far too long. Yes, she talked a good game, saying all the right things in all the right places. She'd heard the words "tomorrow will be better," "move on with your life," and she'd started repeating them, like a parrot learning to speak. The words tumbled through her mind so often that she almost believed them. Almost.

She crossed the room to look upon the comings and goings below. Was Quinn among them, moving through life much as she, there but not?

And then all at once, he *was* there, stepping out of his Jeep as smoothly as silk blowing in a spring breeze. Her heart hammered. Her hand flew to her mouth and then to her head when she visualized the state it was in. She spun in a quick circle and was halted in motion at the sound of the downstairs bell. Her entire body jerked as if zapped with electric current.

Maybe she should just tiptoe back to her bedroom and hide out until he went away. She cupped her hand to her mouth and realized she hadn't brushed her teeth.

The bell rang again. She almost hollered this time.

"Damn."

She took two steps of indecision and a quick sniff of her unwashed underarms. "Passable," she mumbled and stomped barefoot to the intercom.

"Who?" she asked innocently.

"Quinn. Quinn Parker."

Rae squeezed her eyes shut, and pressed the button marked DOOR, releasing the front lock. "Damn, damn, damn."

* * *

Quinn pushed open the heavy wood and glass door and wondered how in the hell he'd wound up in front of Rae's building instead of at the laundry as he'd intended—where he belonged. His plan was to do laundry, the very same laundry that sat in a heap on the backseat.

Slowly he climbed the stairs. What would he tell the woman when she opened the door? What explanation could he offer the inquiring if not offended look she would toss his way? He wasn't sure. The only thing he was certain of was that something stronger than his will had pulled him there. And there was nothing he could have done about this particular itch but scratch it.

He reached the third floor and had a choice of two apartments. Remembering the lights from the night before, he headed for the one facing the front.

Quinn tugged in a long breath, hoped that something that made sense would come out of his mouth, and pressed the square-shaped bell.

Rae jumped again at least an inch off the floor. She stomped her feet as if running in place, squeezed her hands into fists, then reached for the door, with all the poise of a runway model. Her heart galloped at breakneck speed. All she could think about was her disarray, her rumpled clothes and what he would think of her. Why couldn't he turn up when she had her act together, her hair done, makeup in place and the perfect outfit hugging her body?

When Quinn stood before her, bold, black, and beautiful, framed in the doorway as perfectly as by an artist's hand—she couldn't remember why she'd been so afraid. This—whatever it was that was happening between them—was inevitable, as inevitable as the sun setting and the moon rising. And if she thought for a moment that she could stop it, she was a fool.

Chapter Five

It wasn't a dream, Quinten thought as he stood in front of Rae. It wasn't something he'd wistfully imagined. She was real, flesh and blood—full of possibility. Through the night he'd thought of her, heard her poetic voice calling out to him, saw the way she held her head at a just-so angle, her laughter, the sparkle in her eyes and the sadness that could suddenly creep into her voice. She'd haunted him, awakened him with emotions he was certain he was no longer capable of feeling for anyone other than his son; the inkling of joy, the tingle of anticipation.

He pursed his lips before speaking and Rae felt her stomach tumble.

"I know it's not cool to just show up, but I was thinkin' about you. About last night and—"

"It's okay. Come in," she said so gently it sounded like a lullaby to Quinn's ears.

He stepped past her, and the thoroughly male scent of him reached out and caressed her, stroking her body like a tender lover. She almost moaned.

Quinn stepped into the foyer and turned to face Rae, who still stood in the archway.

Soft curves defined the pale blue cotton pants that hung low on her rounded hips, exposing a warm brown belly, with faint traces of the child she once carried. The white band that covered her breasts only drew your attention to them—full, ripe. His manhood jerked, as aware as he. Quinn turned away.

Rae tried to collect herself. But the back of him was just as alluring as the front. His locks, bound in a black band at the nape of his neck, cut a path down the center of his back, in sharp contrast to the white T-shirt that barely contained the cut of hard muscle. The black jeans hugged him in all the right places, outlining the solid thighs and long, slightly bowed legs. Her nipples stood at attention. Slowly he turned toward her.

"I was just getting myself together." She laughed nervously, feeling a sudden pulse between her thighs. "Have a seat. I'll be right back." She headed toward her bedroom, stopped, turned, and collided with his unwavering stare. For an instant she forgot what was on her mind.

He smiled slowly. "Nice . . . place."

Rae swallowed. "Thanks. Would you like something to drink before I dash off?"

"If it's cool, just point me toward the kitchen. I'm pretty handy." He grinned, flashing perfect teeth and that killer smile that graced his book jackets and CD covers.

"Second door on the right."

He nodded. "Thanks."

She watched him saunter toward the kitchen before making a mad dash to her bedroom.

An audible sigh wafted around Rae as she shut her bedroom door behind her. She closed her eyes. Quinn Parker was standing in her living room. Now what was she going to do?

She glanced up and caught a peek at her disheveled self in the dresser mirror. "Oh, Lawd!" She jetted off to the bathroom.

After a lightning-fast shower with her favorite bath gel, some oil spritz for her short twists, a dash of lip gloss for her mouth, she was almost ready. She pulled on an African print wrap skirt that she tied at the waist, and a sleeveless tank top in burnt orange that matched the bold bronzes, emerald greens, and sunshine yellows of her ankle-length skirt. She dabbed some China musk body oil at her wrists and the pulse at the base of her throat.

Rae spun toward the mirror, didn't dare look too long, certain that she would find some flaw, some fault. She hauled in a breath, made a silent vow to play it cool, then stepped back into the front room, fully expecting her surprise guest to be hovering around anticipating her return.

Quinn was missing in action.

Then she heard sounds coming from the kitchen. She eased toward the door, a serious frown on her face, trying to imagine what in the world he was doing.

When she arrived at the threshold, she was taken aback to see Quinn moving comfortably around in her kitchen as if fixing breakfast in her space was something he always did.

He'd prepared a tray of toasted bagels and another

with jelly, vegetable cream cheese, and butter. Somehow he'd found her glass carafe—a wedding gift she thought she'd lost—and filled it with orange juice. The scent of brewing coffee assaulted her senses, and her stomach shouted out in hunger. Rae wasn't sure if she should be pissed off at his audacity in just taking over her kitchen, or totally charmed by his thoughtfulness.

She folded her arms, her braless breasts resting comfortably on them. "I see you found everything you needed." She rested her right hip against the frame in the doorway.

Quinn glanced over his shoulder. "Hope you don't mind. I figured after the late night"—he shrugged—"maybe you took your time about movin' into your morning." He smiled slow and lazy. "Hungry?"

Rae felt the grin spread helplessly across her mouth. "Starved."

"Have a seat. Breakfast is served."

Amusement danced in her eyes as she took a seat. "Are you always this considerate, or is this a new millennium come-on?" Rae quizzed over bites of bagel lathered in cream cheese.

Quinn hooked his legs around the spindles of the kitchen stool, as he leaned over the counter to refill his juice. He chuckled half heartedly. "Tell ya the truth, I don't know. I guess I'd like to think I am a considerate guy. No doubt. Isn't that what you women want these days?" he taunted playfully. "Rugged on the outside with a soft center."

"So this *is* just some fancy come-on," she teased in return, reaching for a bagel and brushing the tips of Quinn's retreating fingers.

Their gazes found each other for a hot instant.

"I guess it's been a while since I did anything for anyone else, or since I cared enough to bother." He lowered his gaze, shielding himself from her.

Understanding that kind of aloneness, the depths to which it could pull you, momentarily sealed Rae's lips. She wanted, as always, for her words to matter. Not give him a pat response from the plethora of self-healing dictums.

"I was working on a new piece," Rae said gently, steering them away from the dark waters. "Would you like to hear it?"

"Sure."

They left the remains of their late breakfast and went into the living room. Lovingly Quinn's eyes roamed across the smooth wood surface of the magnificent piano, the only piece of furniture in the cavernous room. His mouth nearly watered in appreciation for the beauty—knowing the kind of sound that could be drawn from it. To him, playing piano was so much like making love to a woman. You had to know and understand each and every key and what it was capable of doing if touched just right—the high and low notes, the trills that could be emitted with several well-placed finger strokes. It was too intimate, too personal, and he wanted to be neither.

Quinn noticed the pile of body-size pillows stacked in the corners. He walked over and made himself comfortable, half sitting, half reclining like a satisfied cat.

That did it, Rae realized. If there was anything to convince her that this was a man after her soul, Quinn's behavior sealed it. Everyone who'd crossed her threshold always commented about her lack of furniture, the echo in the room, her lackadaisical attitude about "fixing the place up." Not Quinn. He was just as at home as if it had been his. He looked as if he belonged there.

Rae stepped over to the baby grand and took a seat. She glanced over her shoulder. "This is still rough," she said as a preamble.

"Hey, unless you're Stevie Wonder or Prince, it takes a minute to write some music."

Rae chuckled in agreement. "If only," she uttered on a puff of laughter, her confidence boosted by his simple observation.

She flipped the sheets of music to the beginning, pulled in a breath, and exhaled a melody. Her fingers taunted the keys with sharp, sudden chords, played along its spine like a rock skimming water, barely touching but enough to make it ripple. Then her voice slid between jazz and hip-hop, blues and easy listening.

". . . so afraid that time won't erase what I feel for you.

Let me go, you need to know
It's time to move on.
All those yesterdays, memories, and such,
Though they meant so much, they're gone
And I'm all alone.
Let me go. You need to know
It's time to move on.
But I'm so afraid
That time won't erase what I feel for you
In my heart.
I will always remember your smile.
The touch of your hand,
The way you'd walk out a door.
But all that's no more.

Let me go.
You need to know it's time to move on.
But I'm so afraid that even time won't erase
What I feel for you . . ."

It was as if she'd written every word for him, as if she'd seen inside his heart, his soul, and created the words that he dared not speak, Quinn thought, stunned by the effect the lyrics were having on him—stirring images, emotions, dreams long denied. His throat tightened, the warmth flowing through him as he allowed the rhythm of the words to grab hold of him, seep into his pores. He fully understood that they'd seen the same emotions, shared the same fears. And the realization shook him.

". . . What I feel for you will never die.
What we had will always be.
But listen to me
And let me go.
I'll keep you close to my heart
Even if I start . . . to love again . . ."

Rae's strong alto rose to a tingling crescendo, raising the hair on Quinn's arms, swooped down to massage his belly, then gently faded, leaving a whisper of its scent behind.

Rae lowered her head, feeling spent as if she'd just made passionate love. The words had flowed from her unbidden, taking her by surprise, keeping time with the notes she'd created.

Neither spoke, each silently acknowledging the significance of the moment. Everything had just been said.

Rae felt the heat of him directly behind her, tenderly wrap around her to hold her close. She gave in to the embrace, shut her eyes, and rejoiced in the sensation of being held by someone who truly understood.

"Have you let go?" Quinn asked in a ragged whisper, coming around to sit beside her, not fully understanding why he'd suddenly held her like that. But he seemed to need the contact of warm flesh against warm flesh as much as he believed she did.

"Some days are better than others."

"Yeah. No doubt." He dragged in a breath and found her eyes, which had filled with tears that flowed onto her cheeks. With the pad of his thumb he gently brushed them away.

Rae smiled weakly. "Why are you here, Quinn?" Her eyes dragged over his face, memorizing the contours, the sweep of his brows, the depth of his dark eyes, the perfect symmetry of his lips, the smooth chocolate of his skin. She wanted to touch him, taste him, have him hold her again, and her hold him back. She wanted to lie with him, have his fingers awaken her flesh. She wanted to feel him inside of her, if only for a moment, just long enough to remember what it felt like to be a woman. She hadn't wanted that with anyone for so long. Couldn't bear the thought of a man other than her husband touching her. But Sterling was gone. She was still here. She was still alone, still afraid—even now when the man who'd made her blood heat again was mere inches away. And she didn't want to be those things anymore—alone and lonely—at least for a few precious moments.

"I'm not sure why I came, Rae," Quinn finally answered. "All I know is that I couldn't stop thinkin' about you all night. I woke up this morning and you were here." He tapped his temple. "Right there in my head, messin' with my mind."

There was a sense of wonder on Rae's face as she watched him confess. She'd felt the same way—all night, as she'd walked the floors and the music taunted her. "I didn't expect this."

He laughed self-consciously and tossed it off, getting up and moving away from her. He walked to the window, keeping his back to her, gathering his emotions back into the tight band that held them in place and out of reach.

"What do you want from me?" she asked gently.

He hesitated a moment, not sure of just how far he wanted the door to be pushed open. "I don't know. Maybe everything—too much. Maybe nothing. I don't know if anyone can give me what I'm looking for."

"What *are* you looking for, Quinn?"

"Peace, absolution, my soul back." He took a breath, exhaling. "I'm just tired. . . ." He pressed his hand against the window frame, bracing his weight against it.

"Tired of what?" she asked stepping up behind him and placing a hand on his stiff shoulder.

"Tired of hurting inside," he answered wearily. "Tired of feelin' I got a raw deal from life." He moved out of her reach. The door had been pushed open too far.

Rae watched him, trying to see what he was trying

so desperately to hide. Was he like the others who came at her with soft, sweet words, promises, and damaged souls, expecting her to heal them? She wondered if Quinn was worth the trouble. Something unnamed told her that he was.

"I've been there," she confessed. "Still there at times. But we find a way to move on."

"By what, forgetting?" He turned toward her, his eyes suddenly dark and dangerous.

"I don't have all the answers. I may never have them. All I can believe in is that healing takes time. It'll happen for you." She needed to believe that as much as he did.

His jaw clenched. "What makes you think you know so much about me?" he demanded, suddenly irrationally angry, defensive.

"Your eyes," she said simply, unafraid of his unwarranted attack. "It's all there. The windows to the soul." She smiled softly and crossed the room, sat down on a pillow and continued. "If you ever decided to play again, it would be there as well. And that's not always a bad thing. Listen to the blues. It's the heart of ache and loss that gives it the richness and depth, which makes it touch something inside us." She wrapped her arms around her knees staring into his stormy eyes.

Quietly he appraised her, and realized why he was so angry with her. He was afraid of her, afraid of her ability to see beyond his shell, to peel it away and expose him. And his greatest fear was that they would both discover that there was nothing inside.

"Do you ever think you'll play again?"

"I don't know," he answered in a monotone.

"What are you afraid of?"

The question shook him. *How could she know?* He swallowed, fighting down the seed of truth that struggled to burst forth. He failed. "Myself," he answered. "And you." He came toward her.

This time it was Rae who moved away to safety—out of reach, wary almost, rising to circle him as her emotions raced. Finally she stood still, gripping the edge of the piano for support. Her gaze connected with his. "So am I," she whispered.

Quinn stepped up to her, absorbing all the available air in the room. She suddenly felt light-headed. He reached out to her, gently stroked her cheek. "What are we going to do about it?"

She looked up at him. "Maybe stop being afraid." Her body trembled beneath his touch.

"How?" he asked, his soul desperately needing to hear the answer.

"Through the fire—to the safety on the other side."

His very own thoughts again, he realized. "I don't know if I can."

Rae took his hand in hers, and smiled tenderly. "Neither do I, Quinten Parker. Neither do I."

And in that instant they found themselves in an unfamiliar place, a place long forgotten—filled with promises and truths unspoken—the future.

Chapter Six

The studio session was in full swing. Quinn had run out of excuses for not getting there as he'd promised and finally found himself seated on the opposite side of the sound proof room, watching them do their thing. Funny, how Rae had wiggled her way into his life, with him kicking and screaming all the way. The truth was, he kind of liked it. Liked the feel of being part of something, sharing, even if it was only a bit of himself. At least it was a start. Who knows, maybe it could really turn into something if he let it.

It all seemed so easy, too easy, Quinn mused as he absently tapped his foot and nodded his head to the beat of the band. He and Rae had fallen into a comfortable pattern of spending time together during the past two months. They'd talk on the phone, or meet for drinks in the evening, sometimes even did laundry together. He checked out some of her performances, and they hung out at some of the local spots every now and then. The only problem was, it seemed that she was always surrounded by people: the band, girlfriends, studio folks. And they all wanted to get in his business, find out what the deal was with him and Rae, when he was going to play again, write again. He didn't even know. At times it really pissed him off. All he wanted was to be left alone, not become a source of conversation for her curious friends. But a part of him understood. He had his aloofness as a buffer against the world and she had people and her music. Hey, whatever. He wasn't about making waves anyhow. That's why he stayed away. This was her world, not his anymore. And if she hadn't practically begged him, he wouldn't be sitting there now. But she couldn't seem to understand that, couldn't seem to understand what it did to him.

He watched her do her thing behind the studio glass, directing the band, switching up on the music. He had to admire her, though, her drive and focus. In that way she was a lot like Nikita. But the similarity ended there. Rae was her own woman. She wasn't born into privilege, hadn't attended Ivy League schools, didn't surround herself with people who looked down their noses at others. Rae wasn't trying to get on the other side of the tracks to see what it was like. She lived there. She'd made her way through life on her own, without anyone's help.

One evening over dinner she'd told him where and how she'd grown up and even he was amazed that she'd survived.

"There were five of us," she said, sipping her screwdriver. "Me and four brothers."

"Where do you fit in?"

"The oldest." She laughed lightly. "And believe me, being oldest in my house had no perks, especially being the only girl."

"Why?"

"My father—such that he was—believed that a woman's role in life was to take care of the men, no questions asked. And if you did gather up the nerve to question anything, you were sure to get an ass whipping. Maybe get one just because he felt like it at the moment. Me he only beat once a month. My brothers he beat like it was a religious ritual."

"Damn. What about your mother? Didn't she do anything, say anything?"

Rae twisted her lips. "My mother had been whipped into submission years earlier. She wouldn't even speak unless my father said it was okay."

Quinn slowly shook his head, knowing that there was nothing he could say to make it all disappear, be different somehow, so he just listened.

"The minute I turned sixteen I left. Got on a train from Mississippi and came to New York. I never looked back, too scared I'd see my father running up behind me." She shivered at the image. "Found a job as a waitress in Brooklyn and finished school. I had this great music teacher who took a liking to me. She got me into the high school choir. I used to stay after school and watch her practice on the piano." She glanced up at him. "That's how I learned to play."

The corner of his mouth curved up into a grin. "So did I. Just listening mostly."

Rae nodded in understanding. She took a breath and another swallow of her drink. "When I graduated, Ms. Granville, that was her name, told me about a small recording studio in Bed-Stuy in Brooklyn and a guy that was looking for talent. So I went to see him, not knowing what to expect, but hoping he'd miraculously make me an overnight sensation."

They both laughed.

"That brother worked me to death. Do you hear me?" She chuckled, remembering the countless nights of burning the midnight oil. "RJ was no joke. He taught me so much about the business, introduced me to people, and did my first demo for me. When I met with the producers at Sony, they loved what they heard and wanted to sign me right then and there."

"I hear a but in there somewhere."

Rae grinned. "But . . . I didn't want to sing, never did. I wanted to write and compose."

"So what happened?"

"I told them I wasn't interested. Well, RJ almost had a stroke right in the office. He'd worked for three months to get me in. If looks could kill I would have dropped dead right on that plush red carpet."

Quinn howled with laughter. "Woman, you are crazy."

"Yeah, they thought so, too."

"So what happened?"

"After the producer cussed RJ out for wasting his time, RJ begging and pleading with him, I did something I'd never done before in my life—opened my mouth and said what it was that I wanted, for once. Not what someone else wanted for me.

" 'I want to write music, lyrics!' I shouted over the din. They both turned and looked at me like I was crazy. And suddenly the old fear of being beaten took hold of me and pushed me back down into my seat. The room grew deathly quiet.

" 'What did you say?' the producer asked.

" 'I want to write.'

"He leaned back in his seat.

" 'What makes you think you can?'

"I reached into my bag and pulled out my notebook that I'd been writing songs in since high school and handed it to him. I swear he must have read it for an hour, or at least it felt like it, especially with RJ cutting me dirty looks every few seconds. Finally he put the book down and closed it. He stared at me for a long time.

" 'I have a young girl group. They have talent but their music sucks. I want you to listen to them, see if you can come up with something, and then we'll see. Maybe one of these songs.' He tossed the book back at me and my music career began."

"Did you get to work with them?"

Rae nodded.

"Did they take off or what?"

She nodded again.

Quinn cocked his head to the side, realizing he was going to have to pry the information out of her. "You gonna tell me who, or what?"

"After Five," she said shyly.

He tossed his head back and laughed in awe. After Five had jetted to the top of the charts and remained there for years. Most of the girl groups of the past ten years had been patterned after them. *Unbelievable.*

But that was Rae, cool and unassuming, Quinn thought as the music came to an end. He often wished, especially after meeting her, and being plunged back into the world of music, that he could find that creative part of himself that he'd lost. Somehow she was able to hold on to that part of herself where he could not. In his mind, the whole creative process was connected to his past, a past that he wanted to forget, but couldn't. He didn't know if he ever would.

The session ended and the band started filing out of the soundproof booth. There seemed to be a glow, a radiance about Rae as she walked toward him. Oh, how well he remembered that feeling. The rush.

"So what did you think?" she asked on a breath, dropping a headset around her neck.

"Sounded great."

She tucked a lock behind his ear. "Really?" Her finger stroked his chin. She needed to hear his words of assurance to usher out her doubts.

"Yeah, really." He smiled, wanting to pull her close, but didn't.

The tightness in her chest slowly eased. "Well, that's it for today. I'm beat. Let me just tie up a few things with the band and we can leave. Want to go over to the Blue Note? Everyone is going."

There was that everyone again. "Naw. I'm gonna cut out. You go 'head with your friends." He brushed her forehead with his lips and turned and left.

Rae watched him leave, and that same emptiness in her heart that she always felt when he moved away from her found its way back and settled. She was falling for him. Hard and fast. It was the only thing she was certain about anymore. Her thoughts were full of him, her actions planned around him. Her work once again had become a diversion, her friends a shield. But this time instead of it all protecting her from pain, it was keeping her from losing her heart.

She couldn't risk that again, especially with a man like Quinten Parker, whom she knew so well, and not at all. He was full of light, dark shadows, and pieces that she could not put together. He wouldn't let her. Then at times he was open, communicative, funny, romantic, and accessible. At others he was as remote as a distant continent.

She sighed and turned away, knowing all her efforts to keep a seal on her emotions were futile. "Listen, I'll see you all later," she called out to the group. She snatched up her bag and dashed out, hoping to catch him before he pulled away.

When she stepped outside she saw his Jeep and she felt that familiar breathlessness take over. Slowly she walked over to where he sat behind the wheel. "Can I get a lift?"

Without responding, he opened the locks and she got in.

They pulled up in front of her building, spending most of the half-hour ride in silence.

"Thanks," Rae murmured and reached for the door.

"I'll call you."

Rae stopped and turned toward him, a sudden realization hitting her as sure as a smack. *This is the way it will always be with us,* she concluded. This netherworld where illusion is the reality, forever locked in place with no hope of more.

"I . . . don't think you should, Quinn. We're simply going through the motions, pretending that all is right with the world. We are never asking for, or expecting, any more than the little we receive, convinced that we are okay." She didn't know when this half-step was no longer enough, only that it was.

He stared at her, knowing that this moment between them was going to happen, and maybe it was best. Better now than before she became too much a part of his life, found her way into his soul. Slowly he nodded, tugging the inside of his bottom lip with his teeth. "If that's what you want."

Rae felt the rage well up inside her, the weeks of frustration and uncertainty. "What about you, Quinn? Do you even know?" she shouted.

"I'm not like you, Rae—"

"I don't expect you to be," she snapped, cutting him off. "You don't even know what you're like. You live this half-life, just going through the motions, pretending to be alive. I'd hoped that we would have moved beyond . . . this . . ." She tossed her hands helplessly up in the air. She took a breath and lowered her voice. "But it's not happening." Her gaze pierced him. "And you know why? Because you won't let it. And I can't deal with it anymore. I won't." Slowly she shook her head. "Good-bye, Quinn." She opened the car door. One foot hit the pavement.

"What do you want from me, Rae?" he ground out from between his teeth.

She snapped her head toward him, stunned by the anguish in his voice. She reached across the gearshift and took his hand.

"I want you to live again, Quinn," she whispered. "I want you to care about life again . . . about me."

He snatched his hand out of her grasp. His voice turned cold, indifferent, his guard going up. "Caring comes with a price. I've paid it once too often."

"Nothing worth having is free—or without risks.

You need to decide if we're worth the risk and if you're willing to take it.'' She stepped from the Jeep, closed the door gently behind her, leaving him with his demons and her parting remarks.

And as Rae walked up the steps to her apartment she wondered when she would ever be able to do what she demanded from him.

Chapter Seven

Quinn lay on his back, hands tucked behind his head, staring sightlessly up at the stucco ceiling. He knew Rae was right, right about everything, right about him. Somehow he'd convinced himself that he could simply glide through this thing between them—no commitment required—without turning over too much of himself to her. Each time he felt the stirrings of emotions rise within him, he'd shut down, shut her out. He wasn't trying to hurt her, he was trying to keep from being hurt. There were parts of him that were dead inside, or so badly bruised he didn't want those sore spots to be touched. He did want to reach out, to be a part of something, a part of someone's life, but he no longer knew how, knew what to do. It was true what she'd said about the half-life that he lived. Sometimes he felt as if he were in some sort of vacuum, moving through the world like a ghost. He could see, smell, touch what was going on but he couldn't be a part of it. Sometimes the loneliness, the bottomlessness was so great that all he could do was weep into a bottle of Jack Daniels, try to dull the never-ending ache that lived with him day in and day out.

Everyone thought that he should be better now. Nikita was gone for three years. He had a son to think about, a career, himself. But none of them understood that it was so much more than the loss of his wife, his sister, his mother, his youth. It was the sum total of it all that had driven the life forces out of him, as surely as rebel troops forcing out the helpless villagers. None of them understood that each of those wounds had never truly healed, but were only bandaged. And each loss stripped away another layer of the wrapping until the wound was laid bare and raw.

What did Rae expect him to do—just smile and tumble in love with her? Maybe it was easy for her, but it wasn't for him. Not again. Yet the only time he felt any semblance of life still beating inside him was when he was with her, when he heard her voice, listened to her laughter, watched her compose. Couldn't she see that?

But even knowing all that, what could he possibly hope to give to a woman like Rae?

His phone rang. Slowly he turned on his side and lifted the receiver.

"Yeah," he mumbled into the phone.

"Hey, Q. It's Max."

He sat up, a frown creasing his brow. "Whassup, Max? Everything cool with Jamel?"

"Yes, he's fine."

His heartbeat slowed to normal.

"Actually he wanted to speak to you." She paused a moment. "He still hasn't stopped talking about his visit to New York to see his *daddy.*"

He could almost see the smile on her face and the tiny gap between her front teeth. "It was special to me, too, Max," he said sincerely.

"I know."

An unspoken understanding hung between them.

"Uh, before I put him on the phone I wanted to talk with you about something."

"Shoot."

"Well, the holidays will be coming up before you know it, and Taylor and I were planning on spending them in New York with my folks. We figured since Jamel will be out of school, he could spend the two-week break with you. I mean if you don't have any plans."

"No, no plans. Sure he can stay." He swallowed. "That would be great Max, really."

She exhaled. "And I was hoping we could . . . all get together while we were there . . . for dinner or something."

"All . . . as in?"

"In me, you, Taylor, and Jamel . . . and whoever you're seeing."

"I'll have to let you know on that one, Max."

"Fine. But at least think about it."

"Yeah. No doubt."

"Um, Jamel is going to have a baby sister or brother in about six months," she said in a rush.

If he'd been standing he would have fallen. A hundred thoughts flew through his head at once, the main one being that he never imagined Maxine as the mother of any child other than his. It was still hard for him to think of her as someone else's woman—wife, even after all this time and everything that had happened between them.

"Q?"

"Yeah, yeah, I'm here." He paused. "Congrats, Max. I'm . . . happy for you. Feelin' okay?"

She giggled. "Just the usual, hungry, tired, and sick." She laughed again. "But Taylor is thrilled."

I bet he his, Quinn thought not unkindly. He'd never had that experience with her, with any woman. A flash of jealousy reared its green head, and the old anger that he'd felt toward her for keeping the knowledge of his son from him resurfaced—the years he'd lost.

"Anyway, it was good talking to you, Q. Here's Jamel."

If there was one thing he remembered about Maxine, she knew how to drop the bombs.

"Hi, Daddy!"

At the sound of his son's voice, all thoughts of worry and regret drifted to the background, at least for the time he listened to the escapades of a six-year-old who still didn't have a care in the world. But after the conversation, Quinn grew increasingly restless, pacing the confines of his duplex apartment like a hungry, caged tiger. It was nearly midnight. He was too wound up to sleep and couldn't stand the silence of being with himself any longer.

The avenues were still teeming with activity even on a Wednesday night. He drove aimlessly for a while with no particular destination in mind. He stopped for a light and noticed the sign for Encore. People moved in and out, laughing and talking, some forming a short line to get in, and he wondered if Rae was inside.

He parked the Jeep two blocks away and walked back, figuring that would give him enough time to change his mind, but he didn't, and found himself seated at a table shortly after. The club wasn't as crowded as it had been on the weekend, only a few tables were filled as others sat at the bar. He placed an order for his standard Jack Daniels and a plate of buffalo wings and was served promptly.

A small jazz combo held center stage, playing a medley of John Coltrane tunes and not particularly well, in Quinn's estimation, but who could? He took a sip of his drink and finished off the last of the wings.

He scanned the crowd, and periodically watched the door, hoping that he'd spot Rae, and hoping that he wouldn't. He didn't know what to say to her. Yet he needed to talk to her, tell her about Maxine and her news, how it made him feel. He frowned at a sudden realization. He'd never told Rae about Jamel, about Maxine . . . about much of anything. It was always easier to listen to her, go along with the program when he felt like it, and keep himself to himself. Sure he talked, but not about his life, or any of the people in it. Just about things—all the things that weren't important.

"Shit," he mumbled under his breath.

"Handsome fella like you shouldn't be talkin' to himself. Need to have a fine woman sitting here witchu," came a raspy voice, reduced to a hoarse whisper from years of booze and cigarettes.

Quinn slowly turned his head in the direction of the intruder, and gradually looked up the length of the slight frame of a woman until he reached her face and rested on her eyes. Something inside him shifted uncomfortably. In the dimness she almost reminded him of someone but he couldn't place her.

She was holding one of those big plastic bins that dirty dishes were loaded into, and it looked to weigh more than she did. "Seen you here once before, with a pretty thing, performs here sometimes. Right?" she asked, adjusting the weight of the bin against her narrow hip.

"Hmm." He didn't feel like talking, especially to her. There was something about her that bugged him.

"I try to notice people, remember faces," she continued, ignoring the fact that she was being ignored. "And I'd never forget yours. Knew somebody who looked a lot like you a long time ago. But that was another life. Always wonder how he's doing, though, what became of him."

Quinn looked up at her, the sudden melancholy of her voice catching him by surprise. He tried to make out her features in the dimly lit room, but couldn't.

"Well, you have a good evenin'." She ambled off, and Quinn felt the urge to go after her, demand that she tell him more.

Instead he tossed down the rest of his drink, threw some money on the table, and walked out, thankful for the rush of a cool breeze to lower the sudden rise in his temperature.

He glanced several times over his shoulder, having

the strange sensation that the woman would suddenly leap out of the shadows and whisper something he didn't want to hear. He shuddered and headed for his car. Today was a day he'd rather forget.

But he wouldn't.

Chapter Eight

For a full seven days Rae hoped that Quinn would call. Every evening when she came in from rehearsal she'd rush to her answering machine and check for his message. There were none. Each morning she'd rise and know that today was the day, and each night she'd turn out the lights—disappointed.

She hadn't meant to fall in love with him, but she had. There was no denying it. And the wider the chasm grew between them, the deeper she sunk back into that place she had never wanted to revisit. She'd made several attempts to call him, but backed out, sure that she'd be devastated if he didn't say the things she needed to hear—*Rae, I need you in my life, I want to live again.*

So she buried herself in her music, working grueling hours and driving everyone mad with her demands for perfection, for change, for more. Nothing seemed to work for her.

"What is wrong with you, Rae?" her friend and music partner Gail asked as she sat opposite her at Rae's kitchen table, watching her open and close the fridge, wipe down clean counters, and rewash dishes. "You're acting like someone on the edge, snapping at everyone, working everybody to death. And look at you, you're a mess."

It was Gail who insisted that they cut the rehearsal session short, overriding Rae's insistence that they stay and get it right, not caring how long it took. It was Gail who drove Rae home, determined to get to the bottom of what was going on with her friend.

"Nothing," Rae mumbled, keeping her back to Gail as she wiped down the stovetop for the third time. "Want something to eat or drink?"

"No. What I want is for you to talk to me. I haven't seen you like this since . . . Sterling and Akia."

Rae's back stiffened.

"You did the same thing then, went into a work frenzy until everyone was leery of even being in the same room with you. All you wanted to talk about was work, music, the next project, as if that would somehow make everything go away."

"Well, it did."

"Did it? Really? I don't think so and neither do you. If you're honest."

Those were some of the most difficult days of her life, Rae thought. At the time she was certain she wouldn't survive. "An accident," the police said. You don't lose your family, your life by accident. A simple trip to the local bodega for some sandwiches and sodas had turned into a shootout that left the assailant and her husband and daughter dead.

Sterling Lindsay had been her first love. They'd known each other since high school. She could still remember the first time he kissed her at the senior prom and she knew then and there that he was the man she would marry. He was handsome, kind, generous, and a tender lover.

But she had to admit, they had their problems during their eight years of marriage. Sterling was from the old school that believed it was the man who was the head of the household, the breadwinner, the provider, the decision maker. Her role was simple: be happy, take care of hearth and home. Though he tolerated her musical career, he didn't really support it. They'd had more blowups than she cared to remember regarding her steady upward climb in the entertainment field.

"Why can't you be as proud of me as I am of you, Sterling?" she'd ranted as she tried to get ready for the American Music Awards ceremony. The car was due to pick them up any minute.

Sterling sat on the edge of the bed still in his work clothes, making no attempt to put on the tux she'd laid out for him. He lit a cigarette. *"Of course I'm proud of you,"* he said with a total lack of conviction.

"Then why do we always have to go through this? You make me feel as if I'm doing something so horribly wrong. I love what I do. You know that."

"And what about Akia and me?" he tossed back. *"What do you think happens to us when you spend hours at the studio, come home bone tired, and fall into bed, when you*

travel all over the place behind these so-called artists? You take care of everyone else, Rae. What about us?"

"I love you and Akia," she said, feeling totally helpless. *"What can I do differently? How can I make things better?"*

"Do you really want to know?"

"Yes. Tell me."

"Remember why you married me," he said simply, then got up from the bed and walked out of the room.

She was torn. Torn between her love for her family and her love for her work. She didn't want to give up either. Maybe Sterling was right, she thought, stepping into her gown. Maybe she did put too much effort into her work and not enough into her family. Was she depriving Akia of a real mother, and Sterling a real wife? But she couldn't think about that now. Tonight was too important. They'd work all this out later.

She heard the doorbell and the low voice of her husband when it was answered. She went to the top of the stairs.

"Your car is here," Sterling said and walked away.

She came down to find him in the living room with Akia, seated comfortably in front of the television. Akia looked beautiful in the party dress Rae had picked out especially for the occasion.

"So you're not coming?"

Sterling looked up at her dispassionately. *"No."*

Rae tugged in a breath. *"Come on, sweetie, it's time to go,"* she said to her daughter.

"She's not going either."

Rae opened her mouth to protest, but knew it would be pointless, and she didn't want to argue in front of Akia. He was just doing this to punish her, to make her feel guilty. He never could understand how important her career was to her, how hard she worked to achieve her goals. He would love it if she just stayed home and made babies and had a hot meal on the table every night. But she had a future, and she wouldn't let his jealousy stop her.

She walked over to where Akia was huddled on the love seat. *"Listen, sweetie,"* she began, adjusting her daughter's thick pigtails behind her shoulders. *"Mommy has to go, but I know Daddy has some real treats for you, and you're going to have a great time."*

"Why can't I go?" Akia whined, her eyes filling with tears. *"You promised."*

"I know, baby." She glanced up at Sterling, who stared back at her, daring her to choose. *"I'm sorry. But there will be other special nights. Just me and you, okay?"*

Akia nodded numbly and curled up tighter in the chair. Rae hugged her daughter close, raining kisses on her cheeks until Akia finally giggled in delight. She gave one last look at Sterling and walked out. It was the last time she saw either of them.

Rae breathed in deeply, trying to push the memories away. Slowly, she turned around to face Gail.

"I think I'm in love with him, Gail, and I don't think he can love me back."

"How do you know he can't, or that he doesn't?"

Rae laughed halfheartedly and slowly unfolded the events of the past two months—Quinn's physical presence but emotional distance.

"It's me and Sterling all over again," Rae said. "And what makes it so sad is that for the first time since . . . I began to take a chance on feeling again. I get excited about each day, hearing his voice, watching his face when I tell him about some new music I'm working on. He understands how important it is to me, and at the same time he's turned off by it. And I can't give it up. My music is all I have. It's what keeps me going, breathing almost."

"I hear a but in there somewhere."

"But I still want him, all of him. Not just what's left. And I know there is so much more that he's unwilling to share."

"Maybe unable, Rae. If I remember correctly the news articles said he lost his wife a few years ago, didn't he?"

"Yes, the same time as me. Ironic, huh?"

"Maybe, and maybe it's why you two stumbled across each other. The thing is, you both have found your own way to deal with your losses. You have to admit, Rae, you're single-minded, always have been and became more so when you lost Sterling and Akia. You turned to the one thing that had always been a constant in your life—your work. Perhaps he can't. Perhaps he associates it with the pain in his life and can't or won't deal with it. Men for all their outward machismo hurt a helluva lot more on the inside than we do, and it takes them longer to heal."

Rae was quiet for a moment, thinking back to all the times she would go on and on about what she was doing, how great things were going, and he would simply listen, maybe smile. Every now and then he would ask her to play something, but he'd never come near the piano, as if afraid of getting burned. She couldn't count the number of times she'd asked him to come to the studio or have drinks with her and the band after a session. He'd come twice, and he'd been aloof, almost sullen. Maybe Gail was right. But she believed it was even more than that. What that something was she had no idea.

"What's going on in that head of yours?" Gail probed, seeing the faraway look in Rae's eyes.

"Just trying to put the pieces together. Funny, it was so easy for him to let me go when I told him I couldn't deal with what was going on with us. I told him he needed to make a choice. He chose to let me go."

Gail let the words hang in the air, until Rae heard them herself. *I told him he had to make a choice.* Realization slowly passed across her face and settled. She shut her eyes in acceptance. An image of that last night with Sterling and Akia flashed through her head like a bolt of lightning. *Sterling had forced me to choose.*

"Oh, God," she whispered weakly.

"You have a chance to do things differently this time, Rae, if you really want to. Quinn needs to know how you feel. You need to be honest about that, not just to him but to yourself. Have you slept with him?" she asked cautiously.

"No."

"That's not a bad thing. Cuts down on the complications. Gives you the opportunity to think with your heart and not your body."

Rae smiled wanly. "That doesn't mean I don't want to, believe me. The man turns me on in my sleep."

"So then why haven't you two . . ."

"It's almost like we've been dancing around each other. Being overly polite, while staying on simmer. It's as if we both understand that if we make love it's not about one night. Not for us. And it's scary as all hell.''

Mrs. Finch had watched him over the past week sink back to that place where no one could reach him. She'd heard him walk the floors at night, had seen the hollowness return to his eyes, the look he had when they met, the look he had when he lost his wife. And no amount of running to the supermarket was going to take it away.

''Seems like something heavy on your mind, son,'' Mrs. Finch said, finding Quinn sitting on the stoop staring at nothing. She began to sweep.

''Naw. Not really,'' he said absently.

''Hmmm. It's a sin to lie to an old woman,'' she warned.

Quinn couldn't help but chuckle. She knew him too well. ''So you're callin' me a sinner now,'' he teased.

She flashed him an accusatory look. ''If the shoe fits.'' She swept a perfectly clean spot and scanned the quiet tree-lined block. ''Funny about life, huh? On the outside things seem so plain. But that ain't never the case. Life is complicated, full of twists and turns, surprises . . . people.''

''Yeah, I suppose,'' he mumbled, wondering where this conversation was heading.

''Take you for example.''

Uh-oh, here it comes. He glanced at her. ''What about me?''

''Look how you came into my life. Wasn't under the best of circumstances—after losing your sister and all. But it was right here that your life took a turn. Mine too. At the time, who knew how things was gonna work out? But they did. Always do if you give them a chance and some time. Let folks in.''

She moved toward the gate. ''For every loss something comes along to take its place. It's just the way the world works. But you have to be ready. Or you lose that chance.''

''Sometimes you get tired of losing, Mrs. Finch. Get tired of starting over, picking up the pieces. Ya know?''

''I know, son.'' She turned toward him. ''That's why the Lord sees fit to put folks in our way to help us.'' She smiled. ''If ya let 'em. Life is real hard when you live it alone, Quinten.''

She moved slowly toward him, patted his thigh. ''You'll work it out. Whatever it is.''

He watched her enter the house and wondered if she was as right as she always had been.

''Got some errands for you to run,'' she called out from the doorway, figuring *why not?* ''Seeing as that you apparently ain't got nothing to do.''

Quinn chuckled and slowly shook his head. ''Be there in a minute, Mrs. Finch.''

After cleaning up Mrs. Finch's basement and going to the fish market, the vegetable stand, and the cleaners, Quinn was determined to get out of the house before she found something else for him to do.

He took a long leisurely shower, decided on his black dress pants and matching shirt, and picked up his cream-colored leather jacket as an afterthought on his way out. Although the early days of fall were still relatively warm, the evenings had grown chilly.

He decided to visit his old haunts up in Harlem,

check out Shugs Fish Fry, and maybe pay a surprise visit to his old mentor and surrogate father Remy.

As usual, the streets of Harlem were jumping on Saturday night. Cars were double- and triple-parked in front of the clubs and knots of people stood outside the Lenox Lounge, where portions of the movie *Shaft* had been filmed.

He drove on and pulled up in front of Shugs. The line ran from the front door to the corner. Quinn laughed. Some things never change. He rolled down his windows, and kept driving, letting the night breeze and the sounds of life and laughter join him for the ride. This had all been a part of who he was—still was, somewhere.

Music from boom boxes blared from corners. Transactions exchanged hands from behind tinted car windows and down long, dim alleyways. Tight-knit groups of young wannabes draped themselves over cars and around one another.

Quinn turned on the Jeep's stereo and Miles Davis's "Kind of Blue" filled the air, Miles's lyrical horn sailing above the expert rhythm section. He bobbed his head to the beat. *Miles is the man,* he thought, feeling the music.

Sometimes he missed playing, missed the thrill of walking on stage, the spotlight hitting him, and the applause of the audience, the energy that came from working in the studio, feeling the satisfaction of having your creation come to life. That old familiar longing, which he never seemed able to completely rid himself of, settled in the pit of his belly. Then the melody smoothly segued and for some reason the pianist's touch sounded familiar, a light and gentle touch to the ivories that evoked a sensation of water moving swiftly yet easily along a country stream or even the subtle touch of wind upon autumn leaves. And then he recognized himself in the music from the time when change and challenge forged the ideas, character, and style of his music. "Tumbling," his last album, playing now along the column of his spine, had come from that very place in him. It had come from that part of him, that part that he missed. He was a chameleon then, an artist, ever evolving, who refused to sit still or to settle into any rut just because it was commercial. He missed that. He missed the artist part of himself. Shaken, he eased the Navigator to the curb and parked. For several moments he sat there, eyes closed, letting the music, the memories grab hold of him.

He saw himself as if in a movie, sitting at the piano his sister Lacy had given him, working through the notes, perfecting every line, every bar, all through the night until the sun burst gold and orange above the horizon. Everyone said it was the most brilliant piece he'd done, and that he was destined to take his rightful place among the likes of Herbie Hancock, McCoy Tyner, Bill Evans, and Ahmad Jamal—those who had raised the bar of finger play to another level.

The ballad drew to a soulful close, followed by the easy-listening intonations of Johnnie C, the jazz station's host. "That was the mellow sounds of Quinn Parker's 'Tumbling,' from the album of the same name. Long time since we've heard from the man who put the 'Quiet' in Quiet Storm. We miss you, brotha. And now . . ."

Quinn turned off the stereo, breathing deeply. He looked down at his hands. He didn't even know if he had what it took anymore, if the notes would come, if his fingers would respond.

"Will you ever play again? It's the only thing that keeps me going." Rae's words echoed in his head, her face clear behind his lids.

What did *he* have to keep him going? Anyone who tried to get close he pushed away. All the things that were a part of his life, he'd shut out, cut off.

Rae was right. So was Mrs. Finch. He was only pretending to live. But how could he find a way to make his life real again? Was everything that made him the man he once was so bruised, so destroyed that it couldn't be resurrected? If there were any remnants of the chameleon, perhaps he could find a way to emerge as a new man, a different man. Maybe.

Chapter Nine

It was nearing 11:00 A.M. The members of the band were taking a long-overdue break. They'd been at it since eight that morning. Rae was pleased with the rehearsal session, and was certain they were ready to record the last number. It had taken her nearly two years to write the fourteen pieces that would be burned onto a CD, to find the right combination of musicians and perfect lyrics to accompany the notes she'd woven. The collection was an eclectic blend of sultry vocals and taunting instrumentals that stretched the parameters of contemporary jazz, taking this collection to new heights. But still she felt there was something missing, some final intangible element that kept it a breath away from perfection. She couldn't put her finger on it, only felt it in her mind, in the center of her chest.

Contemplating all possible scenarios, she took a

seat on the edge of the engineering table, hoping to discover what was wrong.

Melvin, the studio engineer, tapped her lightly on the shoulder. "Great session, Rae. The tracks are awesome."

She blinked, bringing the burly young man into focus. "Thanks, Mel. Won't be too much longer." She yawned. "Couldn't have done it without you, baby. You know you're a genius with those dials. You could make anyone sound good."

"Gotta have something to work with, and you definitely have it goin' on. This CD is gonna make you, Rae, believe me."

"We'll see, sweetie. We'll see."

Mel jerked his head over his shoulder. "You got company up front."

Rae frowned curiously and slowly stood, arching her back to work out the kinks. She knew Gail was on a hot date, maybe not to resurface for days, and she hadn't invited anyone. "Who is it? I wasn't expecting—"

"Mr. Q himself," he said with deference in his tone.

Her heart fluttered as a sudden heat flushed her body. She didn't move.

"Whatever happened with him, anyway? He just kinda disappeared from the scene, and the brother was ba-ad, too." He shook his head, bewildered, and reached for a control switch. "Shame. Catch you in thirty. We got the studio until two." He chuckled and started for the door. "Pulled a few strings."

Rae nodded absently. "Yeah, uh, thanks, Mel." She pressed her lips together and tried to think of all the reasons why Quinn would show up here, now, after what was said—what she'd said. She didn't want to hope. Didn't dare. She'd witnessed how uncomfortable he seemed whenever he came to the studio, as if he wanted to run, not walk away. How he almost cringed when someone recognized him, asked him to play, what he was doing, when his next album was coming out. He'd answered in monosyllables as much as possible, or not at all. He'd only come twice, and both times had been at her insistence. Eventually she'd stopped asking him to sit in, stopped asking him to play. It slowly became clear that this was a part of his life that he wanted nothing to do with, wanted the past to stay there. That fact was reinforced to her during her conversation with Gail. So why then was he here? What did it mean?

Pulling herself together, she headed for the reception area. Whatever it was, she'd deal with it.

On the ride over, he'd tried to figure out what he was going to say. Find the words to explain what he'd been wrestling with for longer than he cared to remember. He wasn't sure when the changes in him began: if it was the summer visit with his son, meeting Rae, that older woman at Encore, or the constant infusion of hope that Mrs. Finch fed to him. Maybe it was one thing, maybe a combination that had begun to thaw the ice around his soul. Maybe it was nothing more than time passing—changes happening. The only thing he could be sure of was that he had to start somewhere. He gazed around, remembering the many days and nights he'd spent in a studio just like this one. Maybe this was the start. This place, this step.

"Hi."

The tentative greeting filled him with a sudden warmth that surprised him. Slowly he turned around and when he saw Rae standing there, as lovely as the day he met her, he realized how much he'd missed her—how much more time he'd wasted.

Quinn stood, taking her in, inch by inch: the way the bronze-colored Lycra pants defined the smooth curves of her legs and thighs; the cotton T-shirt that highlighted rather than diminished the swell of her breasts; the sinewy column of her neck, the warm brown of her face, haloed by the springy twists of chestnut hair.

"Hey," he finally murmured in response. He angled his head to the side, looking at her as if she were the only woman in the world. He slid his hands into the pockets of his pants as he slowly approached her.

The room seemed to shrink around them.

Rae held her breath, or maybe it was trapped in her chest, she couldn't be sure over the rapid beating of her heart.

"You look good," he said from deep in his throat, standing mere inches in front of her, forcing her to look up at him.

"So do you."

He shrugged. "How you been, Rae?"

She pulled in a breath, thought about telling him how much she'd missed him, that she was willing to wait for him to figure things out, change his mind about them. That she was sorry for trying to push him. But some buried instinct told her no. That wasn't why he'd come. He was there to unburden himself, to make his own confession in a way.

"Good, and you?" she asked, following her instincts.

"Missing you, Rae," he admitted, his dark gaze unwavering.

Relief widened Rae's eyes, increased the beat of her heart. Her hand trembled ever so slightly as she reached out to tuck that one wayward lock behind his ear. The tip of her finger lingered for a moment near his jaw, gently stroking it.

For an instant his eyes fluttered closed before he took her hand away, pressing her open palm to his lips.

A shudder ran through her and she audibly moaned.

"Can you leave?" he asked in a voice so heavy with something she couldn't discern that it was almost unrecognizable. His free hand cupped her waist.

She thought of all the reasons why she needed to stay. All the work that still needed to be done. This was important, her magnus opus if she did it right, put in the time, made everything perfect. How many years had she waited and worked for today, this time in her life—at all costs? How many hours, days, weeks had she spent toiling, sweating, working out every detail, every nuance, accepting nothing less than one hundred and fifty percent from everyone and even more from herself? And there was still much to be done to get ready to lay the last track. They needed her, couldn't finish without her. She glanced over her shoulder and all that rested and waited on the other side of the control room door—a definitive step toward her musical future. *"Why can't I go with you? You promised."* The tiny voice of her daughter still haunted her. She'd chosen her career over her life once before. It was a deadly game and she'd lost. She turned to Quinn, saw the quiet patience in his eyes—and something else—a faint light of hope—the minute possibility of a different kind of future.

She swallowed, terrified of letting go of the only life raft she'd ever known and reaching out into the dark waters of the ocean, praying that she wouldn't go under. She took his hand and he squeezed hers as if he understood the turmoil and doubt that raced through her head. He was throwing her a new life raft, after the first one had been battered and worn. The decision to cling to it would be hers.

"If you can wait a minute . . . I'll get my things."

Chapter Ten

Quinn stood, watching her inspect his living quarters. "Hope you don't mind that I brought you here."

"No. Not at all." She looked around with admiration at the stylishly decorated living room, the sleek furnishings, original artwork by Biggers, Catlett, Basquiat, and Lawrence. But what drew her like a moth to a flame was the large, beautifully maintained Steinway piano that dominated one corner of the room. Slowly she walked toward it, stroking the polished wood surface of the instrument with reverence.

In the months that they'd been seeing each other he'd never brought her to where he lived. And if she was really honest with herself, in the back of her mind she thought that maybe he lived with someone. At least she did at first. But once she got to know him she understood that Quinten Parker was not that kind of man. If he'd allowed another woman to get that close to him, to penetrate his protective shield, he would never have allowed her to enter his life. It was a matter of respect with him. There was some other reason why he'd never brought her here. Maybe tonight she'd find out.

"This is . . . beautiful, Quinn." Impressed, she turned to him and nearly melted when she saw the half smile and the easy grace of his taut body leaning casually against the off-white wall a few steps from her.

He shrugged. "It's home. Want a drink? Something to eat?"

"Yeah, I'm starved actually. We were working for hours." She tugged on the hem of her sweatshirt.

He tipped his head toward the kitchen. "Come on. Tell me what you want."

No, you're not ready for me to tell you what I want, she thought, following him through the open dining room to the kitchen.

"What do you have a taste for, full-cooked meal, or something light?"

She walked over to the fridge, where he was poised, peering at its contents. Unlike a lot of men, he kept it fairly well stocked, a variety of food for each meal.

"Something light sounds fine," she volunteered.

"Salad?"

"Cool."

"Beer?" Quinn suggested.

"Thanks."

He handed one to her before taking out the ingredients for the salad. Without much fanfare, he put fresh spinach, tomatoes, mushrooms, and cucumbers on the kitchen counter and a flash memory of doing the very same thing with Nikita on her visit that first night ran through his head. But this time, instead of memories of her opening the unhealed wound of her loss, the recollection didn't sting, didn't twist his insides as it usually did. He turned on the water and began washing the vegetables, wondering what that meant.

"There's a big bowl in that cabinet over your head," Quinn said.

Rae handed him the bowl, smiling. "What can I do?"

"Relax. Unwind. How'd the session go today?" he asked, momentarily wanting to live vicariously through her.

"Great. I think." She took a sip of her beer.

"Want a glass for that?"

"No. I'm fine."

"So what do you mean, 'you think'?" He sliced the skin off a cucumber, and glanced at her over his shoulder.

Rae took a breath and tried to vocalize what she'd been feeling. "Well . . . I know the work is good. It sounds great and everyone's loving it. They say it's the best thing I've done."

"But. . ."

"Something's missing, Quinn, and I don't know what it is. It's just a feeling I have. You know?" She looked at him with her brows furrowed.

Quinn put the washed vegetables in the bowl, sprinkled some croutons on top, and placed it on the island counter.

"French or Italian?"

"French."

He took a fresh bottle from the cupboard and placed it next to the bowl. "The plates are on a shelf under your feet."

Rae took out two plates, found forks and knives,

and put them on the counter, convinced by now that he didn't hear her or chose to ignore what she'd said.

Quinn took a seat on the stool. "What do you think it is?" he finally asked, hoping that her answer, any answer would somehow unlock his own mystery, why something that seemed right, remained wrong, untenable.

"The music is there, every note in place, the lyrics move, but . . ."

"But what?" His tone became almost urgent. "Is it *you* that's missing—standing on the outside conducting the orchestra of your life from behind a glass wall?" he asked with the precision of a skilled surgeon.

She looked straight at him as a realization slowly dawned within her. How could he know, understand what she herself had questioned ceaselessly, unless he too had been in that dark space? "*I'm* not there. I'm not anywhere," she confessed, the weight finally being lifted. "It's as if the soul of me has been erased and I'm just going through the motions."

Something inside him opened, shifted, as if a block of ice had been touched by the heat of the sun. He'd needed to hear the words, the words he'd been afraid to say out loud that had danced in his head for three years. He leaned forward, his eyes intense.

"It's the same place I've been, Rae, what I've been feelin'. I can make all the moves, say and do all the right things, and on the surface everything looks great. But inside"—he poked his chest—"it's empty. The melody is gone. Everything seems to lack meaning, any depth."

Her pulse raced as her eyes scanned his face. "Yesss," she uttered, knowing his words had struck home, had found a real truth. "Yes." Her eyes suddenly filled. "How do you get it back, Quinn? I've been fooling myself, fooling everybody into thinking that I was all right, better, moving on. I buried myself in my music, held on to the notes as if they were life preservers that would keep me from sinking. Surrounded myself with people and work, gigs and more work, because I was so damned scared. The music can be a wonderful place to hide yourself inside. It can cloak your fears, provide you with a false shelter. Do you know what I mean?" Tears streamed down her face unchecked.

"Yeah, I do," he replied softly, knowing that secret place quite intimately. Yet, almost jealous of her ability to find refuge there where he had not.

Without further words, she found herself cocooned in Quinn's arms, the strength of him warding off the ghosts that still haunted her, the ghosts that she'd valiantly kept at bay—until now. It felt right, natural. For a moment she could let her guard down, and allow herself to be comforted, protected by someone other than herself. Yeah, she was tired, too.

How long had it been since he'd allowed himself to get this close, beyond the veneer of another person, and let it touch him? He held her and the overwhelming sensation of being needed again, sharing someone else's vulnerability, seized him. It struck him in a totally unexpected way. In the past, seeing their pain without recriminations, without judgment was almost his undoing. That blind empathy often left him without any protective shell, left him without any defenses, opening him to the kind of pain that took years to recover from.

For certain, he had worked hard at protecting himself from the world, from people, being sure that his guard was always up and in place. Maybe it stemmed from the life he'd lived on the street, the unspoken rules of keeping your feelings in check to ensure that they would not be used against you. The unspoken code was that your exterior should never betray your interior. Or as someone once told him, "No one should be able to look at your face and know a damn thing about you or your soul." He had become very good at separating himself from the man he was inside. But how could he merge the two, and finally become whole?

His sister Lacy had always seen through the facade. She knew who he was behind the mask, beyond the posturing. Nikita had tried to do that and for the most part succeeded. She was the first woman to win his heart, but only part of his soul. And that is something he would always regret. There was a part of him that was locked away in an iron box, for which even love, in all its power, didn't have the key. At least that's how it had always been. Now there was Rae, who'd snuck up on him like a mist, like a spirit, found a way to seep into his pores, make him start thinking beyond the moment—and about someone other than himself. But was that enough?

Rae raised her head from Quinn's chest and sniffed loudly. "I feel like such an idiot." She sniffed again, thinking she may have revealed too much about herself too soon, and swiped at her eyes with the back of her hand. As many sisters often said, it didn't pay to tell too much about yourself right away. Some brothers stored all of this info, knowing all of your weaknesses, and then hurled it back at you when the opportunity presented itself. Somehow Quinn didn't seem to be that kind of man. She trusted him, maybe from the moment she first met him.

Quinn reached for a napkin and handed it to her.

"Thanks," she muttered and blew her nose. "I'm sorry."

"Sorry for what—being an idiot?" he teased lightly, lifting her chin with the tip of his finger.

"For falling apart like this. I didn't want you to see me like that." She turned her head away, ashamed now for her blatant display of weakness.

"Like what, Rae? Open, honest with me, yourself? Admitting things out loud that you'd only whisper alone in the dark? I know how hard that can be."

She got up and moved away from him, away from his prying eyes, away from the truth that rang like a church bell at high noon.

Suddenly he saw himself through her eyes, through the eyes of those who had been in his life. His bruised inner self mirrored in her words, her admission. How hard he'd worked to keep his front intact. Seamless. The role, the image was all important at the expense of everything. The words like hot lava boiled in his throat, rising to the surface unstoppable now that the earth had moved, shifted beneath his feet, unsettling everything in *his* world. What he'd feared for so long was about to happen, the splintering of his shield, the exposing of his vulnerable, private self.

"It . . . was my fault," he began in the halting words of a child who'd just learned to speak. "From . . . the beginning . . . my mom . . . my sister . . . Nikita. All my fault."

She turned to him, alarmed now by the carnal

agony of his tone. She remained as still as a portrait—waiting. How could she help him?

He sat down heavily, as the images of his life passed before his eyes like a movie in slow motion, and the powder keg of emotions that he'd hidden from formed an explosive knot in his chest waiting for the match to ignite it. The rising to the surface of things long left unsaid, left unrecognized took the wind out of him and caused him to weaken before her. How would she view him now? What woman wanted some guy with a lot of emotional baggage? He now felt the first pangs of guilt, and maybe shame, but if she was who she said she was, it wouldn't matter. None of it would.

Cautiously, Rae approached, seeing the tightrope upon which she walked and the bottomless canyon beneath her feet should she misstep, lose her balance.

"Say it, Quinn," she gently whispered. "Say the words." Now it was she who needed to hear the confession, to assuage her own pangs of guilt, to free herself, absolve herself.

"I . . . I . . . I . . ." He was struggling to find the right words for his feelings. The strain of his inner battle showed on his pinched face, in his frightened eyes.

She came up behind him, carefully, and gently took his hand. "I know it's hard," she whispered, pushing, needing him to cross the line, to take her with him. "Very hard. But if you're the man I believe you are, you'll confront this . . . if you ever want to be free. Otherwise, you'll be locked inside that place in your head and heart forever."

"Why is all of this so important to you?" he snapped, seeking to steady himself by putting her off balance. "What kind of pleasure are you getting from watching me go through this?"

She was now beside him, looking down at him. "I'm not your enemy. Your enemy is someone else—you. And you can choose to fight it or let it beat you. And I can't imagine you letting anything beat you. Tell me if I'm wrong," she challenged. Her heart pounded as she waited to see if he would pick up the gauntlet she'd thrown.

His hands went to his cheeks as he hunched over, staring at the floor. He knew she wasn't wrong, maybe too right. But could he trust her, trust her enough to let go, take the hand that she offered him? "*. . . the Lord sees fit to put folks in our way to help us . . . if you let them.*" The words of Mrs. Finch whispered in his ear. *If you let them.*

His jaw clenched as if trying to seal the words inside his mouth, and then without warning they poured from him, like welcome rain. "My mother . . . she left me, left us . . . and I was responsible for my sister. I . . . I . . . was all she had, the only person between her and the world. I was responsible for her and I failed her."

"How did you fail her?" she asked softly. "What did you do?"

"I . . . I killed her." He said it so abruptly and with such force, Rae was momentarily taken aback.

"I . . . I don't believe that. You couldn't kill anyone. That's not who you are. That's not the man I see sitting here. What really happened?"

"What really happened?" he tossed back nastily. "I'll tell you what really happened, I did to her what our mother did to us," he said, his voice losing some of its power. "I was responsible, and I didn't do what

I was supposed to do, too wrapped up in my own world, my own choices. I didn't think about her, what she needed. I should have been looking out for her and I didn't do it."

"How old were you when your mother left?" she asked gently.

"Sixteen . . ."

Briefly she shut her eyes, unable to imagine the fear and enormous responsibility that had been heaped on his young shoulders. Though she'd left home at sixteen, it was her choice, not something thrust upon her. "Quinn, you were just a child yourself—"

"I was a man," he ground out. "I had to be—for both of us." His eyes grew dark with the memories of the things he'd done to survive.

Rae could feel the chasm opening between them, the distance. She needed to pull him back before he shut down again, cut her off.

"Why did your mother leave?" she asked, giving him some much-needed breathing space. "Did you ever find out?"

He looked at her, narrowing his eyes. "She had problems, couldn't deal with them or us. I guess she felt the only way to handle what was going on in her life was to walk away from everything. Just split. She was selfish, didn't think about what that one stupid act would do to us, her kids. It messed us up, messed us up real good."

"And you'll hate her for the rest of your life, right?"

"I didn't say that." He bristled. "I deal with it. I don't hate her."

"I think you do and it's poisoning your life," she said. "Hate doesn't hurt anybody but the person who does it. Think about what having these feelings has done to you, to your life."

"I think I've done damned well considering what I've come through," he said proudly. "Hey, I could've ended up like some of the other brothers out here. Lives totally wrecked. But I've stayed on my feet."

"Tell me about your sister," she said, trying to keep him talking, keep the conversation away from her and what she'd nearly revealed about her own demons. "What happened?"

He visibly sagged as though she had sucker punched him. It took several minutes for him to recover his composure. He swallowed hard. "My *twin* sister was killed . . . shot down in a drive-by shooting in my old neighborhood. It . . . it . . . was my fault 'cause she kept buggin' me to move, to find a new place, get out of the neighborhood. And I kept puttin' it off, comin' up with excuses. Then one day she was dead. Gunned down like a common thug. And I could have prevented it all if I had just moved out of there when she asked me to. So you see, *I* killed her as sure as if I'd pulled the trigger."

"Quinn, it's not your fault," she said sternly. "It's fate, chance, destiny, whatever you want to call it. When it's your time . . . nothing and nobody can stop it."

"No." He shook his head.

"No, no what?"

"No, I don't believe that. I was responsible. I let her down."

"I see. So you'll spend the rest of your life hanging on to the guilt like some sort of badge of honor," she goaded. "Is that what it's about? You're better than that. And if your sister loved you as much as

I'm sure she did, she'd never want you to live like this."

He sprung up from the stool, nearly knocking it over. His expression turned into a mask of pain and rage. "You don't know shit! You don't know anything about me, what's going on inside me. Your life is all laid out for you. Yeah, you talk a good game, getting folks to spill their guts. Makes you feel good, don't it? Keeps the light from shining on you, don't it?" He stepped toward her, his nostrils flaring. "What about you, Rae? Huh? Why is it that *you* can't hear the music anymore?"

She turned away, away from the mirror that so easily reflected her soul. He was right. It was easy for her to throw out platitudes, wise counsel, and cliches. And it wasn't that she didn't believe them to be true, but they kept her from dealing with her own issues. "This isn't about me," she muttered weakly.

He stared at her back, at her lowered head, and realization rose and stood between them. "Isn't it, Rae? Isn't this what you needed, what you were really after?"

"What are you talking about? I—"

"You and I are cut from the same cloth, Rae," he said, moving up behind her and taking her shoulders in his hands. He felt her body stiffen beneath his fingertips. "You told me once about walking through the fire. Remember?"

She tugged in a breath and nodded.

"You pushed me through it . . . and you were on the other side—waiting. I'll help you. If you give me a chance. If you trust me the same way you wanted me to trust you."

Slowly she turned to face him, looked up into his

eyes, saw the sincerity, the need, the awakening. The walls of her chest tightened.

"Tell me, Rae," he said forcefully, fully turning the tables. "Tell me what stopped the melody."

"I . . . I." She shook her head.

"Tell me," he said in a harsh whisper, knowing if she denied him this one thing he'd surely retreat to that dark, safe place and never return. Not again.

"I . . . should have stayed . . . home that night." Her voice cracked. "I should have stayed . . ."

Bit by bit she relived that dreadful night that changed her life forever. Changed her forever. It was now her turn to face the bitter truth, to take his place in the core of the heat. She measured out the words inside her head, weighing each one. It was unlike her to surrender such large chunks of herself this way. Control by editing. Maintain the emotion, retain the control, and edit what you say. There was no way she would divulge her entire life story in one sitting. No way. Rae didn't do that. Still, she felt uncommonly comfortable with him, comfortable enough to say more than she usually would.

"All I thought about was me, what I needed," she continued slowly, deliberately. "How important my work, my career was to me. And in the end I lost everything. All I had left was my music, my work. Ironic. But it's not enough to fill the holes, the emptiness, no matter how hard I try."

"Yeah, you've said that, Rae," he said, almost cutting her off. "But what do you mean when you said 'I should have stayed home that night'? That's the heart of it."

She kept her back to him once he started asking those questions, the ones that hurt. "If I hadn't gone out, then my husband and daughter wouldn't have gone to the store and gotten killed. Simple as that." Never before had she dared to say the words aloud. And now that she'd shared the load with someone who truly understood, the weight of guilt and regret was lifted.

"And that's haunted you just like the thing with my sister," he said, finally understanding the connection between the murder of her family and the dry creative well that robbed her music of its vitality, the way his own losses had. "That grief spills over into everything in your life, too, doesn't it?"

"Just like you, Quinn?" she murmured, looking at him now. "Mirror images. We both have our crosses to bear."

"I guess. All I'm sure of is that I can't do this anymore."

"So what are you saying, Quinn?"

He bent down to tie his shoe, a loose lace, but kept talking, then stood. "I don't have any easy answers, Rae. I just know that it's time for a change, and how that happens . . ." He shrugged. "It'll come to me. But I'm through anguishing over it."

It was the look on his face that made her stand there, completely admiring and respecting this new man in her life with a whole new set of feelings. It was a look of strength, steely resolve, and even arrogance. Quinn had showed her more than just his scars and wounds; he'd showed her the iron will that had helped him survive all these years, through some old fires and battles. And he'd survived, a bit battered and bruised, but he'd survived, and so had she. Both of them possessed a toughness so few men, or even women had anymore. Yes, they were survivors. The question now became since they'd crossed that first wall of fire, would they continue to fight the blaze together, or become consumed by the flames—alone?

Chapter Eleven

Rae watched the Jeep until it became a mere speck in front of her eyes. Slowly, she moved away from the window, out of the way of the sun that was making every effort to debut, heralding the start of a new day.

And it was, Rae thought, making her way to the bathroom. She turned on the water in the tub full blast and dribbled some bath gel into the rushing water.

The evening spent with Quinn, or more so, with herself, had truly rattled her, took her someplace she'd never been—deep inside herself, right smack next to everything she'd always been afraid of. She'd stood toe-to-toe with her demons, looked guilt and selfishness in the face, and accepted her role, something she had done everything in her power to keep from happening. Except tonight—tonight nothing was as it had been, for either of them.

She tugged on her sweatshirt and pulled it over her head, and stepped out of her pants, dropping them in a heap with her underwear right behind them. Gingerly she stuck one foot in the tub, and bit by bit slid into the steamy water until it reached her chin.

Sighing, she relaxed and closed her eyes, her mind and body humming. She may have thought a lot of things about Quinn Parker: talented, sexy, handsome, caring. But she would never have thought of him as one who would actually open the door to his innermost spaces. He had. And it was her that he chose to share a part of himself with.

The experience touched her profoundly, understanding that what had happened with him tonight was no easy feat, especially for a man like Quinn, who had always lived with the "image." It may have been something as simple as bringing her to his home. On the surface it seemed like nothing at all—but it was. It was an unwritten, unspoken message to her that he believed he could bring her into a small part of his world. Open the doors. Just as his painful revelations to her had been.

What happened between them tonight created a bond that would not easily be broken. It left her feeling closer to him than she had to any man—even Sterling. The thought, though sad, gave her what she needed to finally be able to let go—to mend.

Leaving had been hard. She had wanted to stay. It was Quinn who knew that tonight was not the night. Not the time, not when they were still so tender. When they did come together, and she knew that they would, it would not be with wobbly legs and tenuous hearts. They would be ready, and she was willing now to wait, because she was certain it would be worth it.

Finishing her bath she languidly went to her bedroom and stretched out across the bed. Usually her first thought in the morning would be getting to the studio, getting to her music. Not today. *Interesting.* For the first time something else took center stage in her thoughts. *Quinn.*

If she'd had any doubts that she was in love with him, they were erased. She knew that loving him would be hard, harder than anything she'd ever done. He was the most complex man she'd ever met. Nothing about him was as it seemed. When he allowed you to see beyond the facade, the brilliance of his soul could bring you joy. And just as quickly as he permitted the vision he could make it all vanish, appear as an illusion that you would fight to experience again . . . and again.

But he was what she wanted. And if she knew nothing else about herself, she knew she could be single-focused and determined. She was determined to win his heart and she understood that it wouldn't be easy. Quinn was a man who turned over his emotions in small doses, if at all. He'd made that clear tonight. In that way, they were the same.

He'd approached the center of her, that part that haunted her, stole the melody. But she'd quickly hidden herself from view, unwilling, unable to face herself in the reflection of his eyes. But he was as tenacious as she, and as he had done, she had bared her soul and he hadn't run from what he'd seen.

She turned on her side, listened to the sounds of

activity on the street below. Closing her eyes, she wondered what he was feeling, thinking. If their evening together had the same effect on him as it had on her. She believed it had. How it would manifest itself only time would tell.

By the time Rae awoke it was nearly noon. And her first thought was of Quinn. She'd dreamed of him as surely as if he'd lain beside her. If she closed her eyes, she could smell his scent, see the soft curl of his lashes that draped the dark, intense eyes, hear the rich tones of his voice that brought to mind the notes played from an alto sax.

She knew he was as shaken as she by what was said between them, and instinct told her he'd blame her somehow for the revelations he'd made—the secrets he'd told. She didn't care. All she wanted, at that very moment, was to hear his voice, assure herself that this thing growing between them, in whatever form it took, was real.

Chapter Twelve

Quinn returned from taking Rae home. They'd talked until the sun was moments away from rising. Both of them were spent, yet surprisingly renewed.

He tossed his jacket onto the couch, and walked toward the window, the events, the words, the confessions of the evening still looming in his mind. He stood poised there, his hands bracing his weight against the frame of the window. As he watched the sun slowly blaze across the horizon, signaling the beginning of a new day, for the first time in longer than he could remember he felt the inklings of hope—possibility.

Tonight was a revelation, not just of Rae and who she was, but who he was and what he was capable of becoming. From caterpillar to butterfly, Mr. Osborne, his old high school science teacher, used to say, comparing the stages of development in humans to those of the insect world. A chuckle passed his lips as he recalled the short, squat man directing a pointer at a chart showing the growth of a baby through young adulthood to a mature man. Just like insects, only harder.

Distracted by the night's recollections, he sleepwalked over to the CD player and put in a disk of Bud Powell's greatest hits, pressed the ON button, and draped himself over the sofa, one leg over the armrest. The music of the bop piano legend washed over him in waves; the emotional force of the cascading notes, the endless surge of inventiveness, the courageous risks taken each time the man's nimble fingers struck the ivories. This was jazz at its best. No matter how fast Bud played, there was no lack of ideas, each phrase clearly articulated, each moment full of drama and excitement. Quinn closed his eyes, imagining how the pianist must have felt to be at the peak of his creative powers, realizing there was nothing he couldn't do on the keyboard.

Listening to Bud's incredible artistry on the tunes "Dance of the Infidels" and "Parisian Thoroughfare," he saw the fierce two-handed attack of the master across the length of the black and white keys in his mind's eye and sighed deeply. Works of genius from a wholly original mind. Then he considered the man's slow yet continuous emotional decline into madness and the gnawing away of his talents by heavy drinking and long sessions of electroshock therapy in psychiatric wards. This was what saddened him. He couldn't let his troubled past do that to him, rob him of his gifts, cheat him of fulfilling his promise.

"Damn, that could be me if I don't stop this thing

before it gets the best of me,'' he said aloud to himself. ''Can't let that happen, can't.''

He walked toward the piano, looked at it for a moment, then sat down on the bench. Something happened. It was as if he couldn't move, as though something inside him suddenly sapped all the power from his fingers. Minutes passed, maybe an hour. Still he hadn't played anything. The music was there in his body, in his head, trapped, unable to come out. He sat there staring blankly into space, his fingers poised just above the keys, unable to descend, to touch.

''Damn it,'' he cried out, tears coursing down his cheeks.

He flicked the dreads from his forehead, bent over, and gave in to the torment inside him. It was the first time he could remember feeling this helpless. Crying didn't help. The tears only reminded him of how far from emotional health he really was, how long the trek back to normal would be.

Wobbly, he got to his feet, walked over, and switched off the machine, and Powell's fleet lines of brilliant sound vanished. Rae, Rae, Rae.

Rae. Was this relationship what he really wanted, what he had intended to do when he'd gone to the studio to see her that first time? She'd pushed him, put him on the defensive, ready to attack his shield. Was he ready to let someone knowingly push all of his buttons? To take him to some place where there was no safe ground? Maybe she was just another woman who enjoyed tormenting men. Watching them squirm. *Stop it. Stop this.* She wasn't the problem; he was the problem. No, he hadn't really wanted to attack Rae, but rather that thing that lived inside him.

The notion to call her crossed his mind but he decided against it. It was too soon. He didn't want to seem too eager, like an overanxious chump. Maybe he already had jumped the gun. But the die was now cast. His sacred home, his apartment sanctuary. Bringing her to his home had been a serious move for him. This was where he and Nikita had lived—loved—as best they could. He'd never brought another woman there, believing that it would somehow violate what he and Nikita had shared. But seeing and feeling Rae in this space hadn't hurt as he thought it would. It felt right. It felt good. It felt like change.

He sat back down, staring at the phone. What was he doing? Why was he obsessing about this woman? The caution light was blinking, *warning, warning, warning.*

As if by magic, the phone rang. He knew who was calling before he even picked it up. *Rae.*

"Hey?" Her voice sounded dreamy, all soft and inviting.

"Hey yourself."

"Did you finally get some sleep?" she asked, stretching.

"Naw . . . too worked up to sleep."

"I took a bit of a nap. But I can't rest." She paused, taking a chance. "I thought that maybe we could go out and do something tonight."

He was still feeling the aftereffects of their talk earlier. "I don't know. I don't know if I'm up to people right now. I've got a lot in my head."

This was what she was afraid of, his retreat. But she wouldn't give up that easily. "Getting out among some folks might do you—both of us—a world of good. Think about it, Quinn. No pressure."

"Yeah, right, no pressure," he repeated with some edge to his words.

"Are you upset with me about something?" she asked, unsettled by his cool tone.

"Should I be?" he shot back, not willing to let her see how much their night had affected him. "Look, I don't feel especially social right now."

"Let it go," she said. "You're making much too much of everything. Just let it go." She couldn't let him escape, retreat again, not now, not after it was he who threw her the life preserver, with the promise of keeping her afloat.

"Maybe that's easy for you but not for me," he said, allowing his irrational anger and emotional confusion to erect a protective wall around him.

Had she been wrong in her conclusions about what happened? Did she want this so bad that she was seeing things that weren't there? "I . . . I don't get it, Quinn. You seemed like you wanted to talk and once we do, you turn it around like *I've* done something to you?"

"Maybe it's not about you, Rae."

His tone, his unwarranted attack stung as sharp as a slap. *Fine, if that's the way he wants it.* "Look, I'll be at Encore, if you decide to come, it's on you, okay? A friend of mine is playing tonight at nine. You might enjoy it. Think about it at least."

"Yeah," he mumbled as he heard the phone click in his ear.

Absently, he scribbled down the info, hung up the phone, and walked back to the piano, where he stood staring at the keys for what seemed like an eternity.

Rae. She refused to let him hide, to sink back into his safe place. Damn her! It was so much easier before when he didn't care. The slip of paper was still in his hand, burning his fingers. He stared at it, thought about tearing it up, and did.

Chapter Thirteen

Striding briskly through the light drizzle, along the tree-lined avenues of the West Village, Quinn tried to remember if he'd parked his Jeep on the right side of the street for the following day. He hadn't really been paying attention, his mind focusing on the evening ahead. But the last thing he need was another ticket, that would be four in the last three months, all for parking. He thought about turning back, just to check, but glancing at his watch he knew it would be pointless and just another stalling excuse to keep him away a few minutes longer. He'd just have to take his chances.

Encore. He casually entered the room, looking around to see if she was already there, which she was—seated in a far corner at an intimate, cozy table.

Rae. She looked even lovelier than she had the last time they were together, dressed in a stunning black silk blouse with a red scarf covered with artfully done African designs, tossed around her long neck with a sense of high style. A tall brother, wearing a long straw yellow Arab robe with a shiny bald head and an earring in his left ear, was standing near her, whispering something that seemed to crack her up. She laughed, her head back, all of her bright white teeth on display. It was clear to him that life moved on as usual for her. Rae's laughter didn't stop once Quinn stepped up beside the man, who stood up straight and moved to leave before Rae touched his arm.

"Amir Allie, Quinn Parker," Rae said, making the introductions.

Amir's eyes momentarily sparked in recognition. A broad smile spread across his face. "*The* Quinn Parker?"

"The one and only," Rae said proudly, smiling up at a somber-faced Quinn.

"Glad to meet you, brother," Amir said, smiling, shifting the chew stick in his mouth and taking Quinn's outstretched hand and pumping it between both of his. "Man, Quinn Parker," he said with deference. "Brotha, you can play some ivories. I only wish I had your skills."

"Thanks," Quinn mumbled, becoming increasingly uncomfortable, knowing by rote the direction the conversation would take. Knowing the next string of questions before they were asked.

"Yeah, man, where you been? Back in the studio working on your next platinum, right?" Amir went on. He patted Quinn on the shoulder as if they were the best of friends. "Read that book of yours, too.

Heavy stuff. Brothers don't usually write like that, but I dug it. You're one of those rare renaissance men."

Rae monitored the tight expression on Quinn's face, the look of one who wanted to escape in his eyes. The muscles of his jaw worked up and down, and she realized that he was close to snapping.

"Amir always was a talker," Rae cut in, clasping Quinn's bicep and feeling the tension. "If we let him he'll talk us to death. Don't you have a set to get ready for?" she asked, making her voice light.

"Yeah, yeah, you're right," he said as if suddenly remembering that fact. "Listen, maybe we can talk after my session. Love to hear your thoughts on my set. Most of these folks in here don't know the difference between Monk and Liberace." He laughed at his own joke. "Anyway, thanks for coming."

"Yeah," Quinn mumbled, watching the man walk off toward the bar that lined the wall opposite them, then stopping to speak to the brown-skinned woman, the same woman Quinn had seen here before, who kept staring in their direction. Her stare was making Quinn uncomfortable so he switched seats with Rae so he didn't have to look at her. The place was packed once again but their table seemed to be getting all of her attention. She made him uneasy the way she looked at him, the sound of her voice, the way she seemed to want to touch him.

"You made it," Rae said, moving the lit candle on the table so she could see Quinn's face without its obstruction, and pulling him away from the dark turn of his thoughts. "I didn't think you were coming. You sounded . . . anyway . . . thanks for making the effort."

"Yeah," he said absently, motioning to the waiter. "What are you drinking?"

"Red wine, French," she replied, looking at him with concerned eyes. "Are you okay? You look tired. I'm sorry about Amir. I didn't think he would go on like that. I know how that kind of stuff bugs you. Is that what it is?"

She was looking at his face, the skin drawn taut to the bone and the dark circles under the eyes. The slight signs of wear took nothing away from his handsome face, only enhanced the ruggedness of his masculine features. It was the face of a man who was living life, struggling with its challenges, and occasionally getting the upper hand. Whatever damage had been done could he erased with a couple of good nights of sleep.

"Yeah. I'm all right," he said, still trying to get the waiter's attention. "Forget it. Just tired like you said."

Finally, the waiter came, apologetic about the delay in service, noting that the café was especially crowded tonight. Two tourist buses brought a load of people from some midtown hotel, Japanese and Korean visitors looking for a safe bite of the Apple, all curiosity and cameras. Their heads swiveled from one sight to the other, trying to take everything in at once.

After the waiter brought Quinn's drink, a shot of Jack Daniels, he disappeared but quickly returned to refresh Rae's glass and laid two menus on the table. He stood at the table, waiting for their order, seeming quite peeved when they requested salads rather than meals. Quinn didn't want anything because his stomach was acting up. Had been since their little talk hours earlier. Rae, on the other hand, was watching her waist line, staying away from anything with too many calories, especially after sunset.

"What's the deal with you and Amir?" he asked, an edge to his voice, wanting to find something out of place.

Rae frowned at the accusatory tone. "An old friend. Plays piano. He sometimes backs me at auditions, rehearses with me. Nice brother, a little eccentric. But sweet, loyal, and sincere. Studied at Juilliard for about three years but didn't do anything with it until now. He lived in Africa for about ten years, teaching and learning about their native music. You should see his collection of native African instruments, incredible stuff, some of it's probably priceless."

She finished talking, drank her wine, and drummed her fingers on the table, trying to figure out what was wrong with him. "Are you still upset with me about last night?"

He sniffed, wrinkling his nose. "You got me to talk but when your turn came, you gave me the short and quick version."

"What do you want to know? Ask whatever you want."

"All right," he said, raking his fingers through his dreads. "What about your husband? What kind of guy was he? Did you love him?" he quizzed, firing the questions at her.

She sat forward, then took a long swallow of the wine. "Sterling was a good black man. He'd been through his share of women before we met. Lots of them. When he met me, the first thing he told me was that he wasn't really big on commitment. That shook me because I knew right away that I felt something for him. He said he refused to get serious with anyone because he didn't want to play the games that went along with maintaining a relationship. Women were playthings for him. He told me that he went back and forth between four different women at the same time he was courting me. But he cut them loose when we started to build something between us. In so many ways, he was probably the most honest man I ever met."

"But did you love him?" he demanded to know, as if the answer somehow held a magical key to what ailed him. He drank some more of the Jack Daniels, wincing at the burn of it in his throat.

"Yes, I loved him very much," she said. "When we married, we both did a lot of growing up together. I think we learned that love came with a big responsibility. Loving him was easy. He was caring, thoughtful, and kind. Had a big heart, the biggest. You don't find those combinations in a man, in anybody, too much anymore."

"You make it sound like it was so perfect," he said sarcastically. "Ain't nothing perfect," he added, thinking of the battles he and Nikita had waged. "What messed up your postcard?"

She felt the sting of his words, knew he was goading her, and realized how he must have felt when she was coming at him like this, hard and heavy with the questions. Now the shoe was on the other foot and it didn't feel good at all. He was testing her. Was she able to take it as well as give it?

"Our problems were with his family," she said, still skirting the whole truth. "His parents, mostly his mother, didn't think I was good enough for him. And he loved them almost to a fault, would have done anything for them. He was always trying to earn their love. They didn't treat him like they cared much about him but he loved them unconditionally."

"What did they do to him?" He glanced over her shoulder and saw the woman staring at him. If she kept this up, he was going over to the manager and complain.

"His mother always drummed into his head that he could have done better . . . in every area of his life: his job, his home, me. Making him feel worthless and constantly needing to prove himself. I think that's why he ran around with so many women. Just to boost his ego." Why he felt the need to control her life, make it seem unimportant, she thought but didn't say.

"How long were you guys married, you and Sterling?" he asked, waving to the waiter for a refill.

"Eight years," she said. "Eight good years," she added, trying to convince herself.

"What about your daughter, Akia?"

She swallowed hard and finished her wine in two gulps. "Akia . . . was only five years old. My baby."

In her mind, she recalled Akia as an infant wrapped in a blanket, touching her little pug nose with the tip of her finger, making her smile and gurgle with glee, sitting, just the two of them before the fire. The most blissful feeling in the world. Mother and child. Holding a tiny life you created, a life that depends on you and loves you without asking for anything in return. Her intoxicating infant smell. Her Akia.

Quinn saw the pain in her eyes, knowing that he'd pushed too far. And the satisfaction that he thought he'd feel at seeing her as miserable as he, wasn't there.

She turned away, keeping the memories to herself.

"Hey, I'm sorry. And I'm sorry about the other night."

"You shouldn't apologize unless you really mean it." She kept her face averted as the room suddenly filled with applause, halting any further conversation.

Amir, now dressed in an all-white, blinding tunic and ballooning harem pants, walked out on stage and sat on a stool before a black lacquered Yamaha piano. The lights went down and a small pin spot illuminated the keyboard. He bowed toward the crowd, smiling like a lottery winner, then told them that he would be playing a melody of six Duke Ellington classics tonight. Solo piano. A truly hard gig. A musician out there alone, with no support, just the instrument and his ideas. Someone in the audience squealed when he opened with the Billy Strayhorn composition "Chelsea Bridge," capturing all of the muted colors and haunting harmonies that Duke's right-hand man meant to be heard. Rae leaned over and whispered to Quinn that it reminded her of a piece the classical composer Ravel would have written. He nodded although he was never a big fan of the man.

As if to top himself, the next tune Amir performed was Ellington's "Black Beauty," something he wrote back in 1928. Only Quinn knew that the pianist tossed in notes from Lawrence Brown's original trombone solo on the number. He was impressed. Next Amir played the Master's "Warm Valley," complete with the hornlike voicings of Johnny Hodges, followed by a short but lively rendition of "Caravan," then a longer version of another Strayhorn tune, "Passion Flower," which had the crowd screaming and stomping their feet.

"He can really get down," Quinn said, nodding

his head in appreciation. "You can't judge a book by its cover."

"What does that mean, Quinn?"

"Nothing," he answered, pushing back his chair and standing. "I'm going to the men's room. Be right back."

He maneuvered between tables and chairs in the semidarkness, stepping over outstretched legs, slipping through tight spaces until he made it to the rear of the room. Walking down the hall, he noticed the slight woman with the burning eyes again, staring at him, coming his way. Something in him clenched in the pit of his stomach. Who was this woman? What did she want with him? All this staring and mess. What was her problem?

Ordinarily, he wouldn't have done it. But he did. He strutted up to her and asked why was she staring at him. Standing so close to her again gave him that same strange feeling from before. It was odd that he would feel like this about a woman he didn't know. Whatever it was, he couldn't seem to shake it. A tightness, like a closed fist, now in the center of his chest.

"I don't mean to make you nervous but you look just like someone I used to know," the woman said, glancing at him with veiled eyes. "Just like how he might look now."

"Who?" Quinn asked, suddenly feeling pity for the woman.

"Don't matter . . ." Her words trailed off as if she was about to collapse into tears. "I promise I won't bother you no more."

"When is the last time you saw him?"

Her head lowered toward her chest, a heavy gush of air left her. "Not for a long time. A lifetime."

He turned, stepping aside to let one of the waiters pass with several trays of food, but when he pivoted back around, the woman was gone. Vanished. Gone without a sound like a troubled spirit. Or a ghost. That spooked him for a moment. He glanced up and down the corridor, completely rattled, but there was no sign of the woman.

After his trip to the men's room, he came back to the table with a odd expression on his face, which Rae noticed and asked if everything was alright. He nodded and motioned to the waiter for another refill of Jack Daniels.

"Do you really think you should have another one if you're going to drive, Quinn?" she asked, placing her slender hand over his big one.

"Hey, lighten up," he snapped. "I can handle it."

Stung, Rae pulled her hand away.

Both of them looked at the stage to hear Amir introduce his last number, "Take the A-Train," which got the crowd revved up again. He danced around the well-known melody on the keys, dissecting it, teasing it, twisting it into an even grander version of itself. If that was possible. Its passages now carried a bluesy feel, then a majestic shouting gospel mood and finally it morphed back into its original shape. And that brought the crowd to its feet cheering.

Quinn was still trying to get the attention of a waiter to get another drink. The waiters were huddled in a corner, talking among themselves and clapping like everyone else. *What the hell is wrong with everybody? Can't a man get served properly?*

Before Rae knew it, he was up and marching angrily

through the tables. She watched him with the waiters gesturing wildly back toward the table, his mouth moving a mile a minute. What could he be so mad about? One of the waiters began walking away from Quinn and he followed, still talking and motioning with his hands. Finally, Quinn returned.

Once back at the table, he sat quietly fuming until Amir left the stage and the lights came up. The waiter brought his drink, serving him but rolling his eyes the entire time. Quinn said nothing. His mind seemed somewhere else. Rae watched him silently, watching the storm of emotions swirl across his face. She wanted to ask him what was wrong. Wanted to get into his head. But she wasn't sure if she was ready to handle what she might find there.

He killed half the drink in one swig. He glanced at her sideways, and blurted out something. The noise in the place was deafening. You couldn't hear yourself think.

"What did you say, Quinn?"

"You said you had a daughter . . . and I said I have a son." He almost shouted it so she could hear him above the noise of the drinkers and laughers.

A son? "I didn't know you and Nikita had a child," she said, warily. "How old is he?"

He was determined to get it all out. "Nikita's not the mother. Someone else is the mother, another woman."

"Another woman?" she asked in confusion. "Who?"

"Maxine. It didn't work out."

What had she walked into? Another woman with his child. Where were they? What was his relationship with this Maxine he alluded to so casually? She had a million questions but couldn't get them together to ask.

He was staring at his drink, looking down into the glass. "My son's name is Jamel. He lives on the West Coast with his mother. She married some guy."

A momentary wave of relief. "Did you love your son's mother?" she asked, looking him in the face.

"I don't want to talk about this anymore," he said, a bit wobbly, standing. "Let's get out of here. I need some fresh air."

He paid the waiter, walked toward the door with Rae a step behind him. Had he stopped to consider Rae's feelings—shock, surprise, doubt—he may have handled the disclosure of his son's existence a lot differently. Instead, he got buzzed and blurted it like a tattletale before a glum teacher. Inside, he knew this should have been handled with much more finesse and grace. But at the moment he didn't care. All he could think about was shocking Rae, upsetting her balance to see if she would stay or bolt. Tomorrow, he'd feel even worse when he really thought it through. He kept walking through the doors, past the bouncers, to the street. Rae was right behind him—*staying.*

When he looked back at the place, there, in the shadows of the entrance, stood that woman. The look in her eyes would remain stapled in his mind for the next week, haunting him, triggering feelings that shook him to the core of his being.

Chapter Fourteen

Rae stole furtive glances at Quinn from the corner of her eye. His profile was intent, rigid almost. He'd been edgy and short from the moment he'd walked into Encore, and she wondered why he'd bothered to come at all, if what he'd intended to do was brood.

And then that woman. She frowned. She didn't know what was going on there, but it shook Quinn up to a point that he said he was ready to leave. She seemed harmless enough, just a lonely, late-middle-aged woman trying to make a living and pass the time chatting with customers.

"Are you all right?" Rae asked again for the tenth time.

Quinn rolled to a stop in front of her building. "Yeah, I'm cool."

She pushed out a frustrated breath. She had no

clue how to get through to him if he wouldn't talk to her.

"Fine," she said a bit sharply and opened the passenger door. "I guess I'll talk to you later . . . or not." She got out and slammed the door behind her, her temperature rising with each step she took.

"It's not worth it," she fumed, pacing the floor of her apartment, as she tossed her jacket in the corner, her ankle-length boots in another. She pulled off her black silk blouse and stomped toward her bedroom. "He stops me at every turn, slams doors in my face, cuts me out, then blames me for how he feels." She flung open her closet door and snatched out her robe. "Why is this only about him? What about me? Why the hell can't he see that I hurt, too, that I need, too?" Tears filled her eyes, but she refused to cry. Not anymore, not over Quinten Parker.

How could she have been so totally wrong about him, about them? She was playing a naive game with her heart, and she'd lost big time. It was clear that Quinten Parker was content staying exactly where he was in his life. She glanced up in the dresser mirror, truth reflected back at her. And so was she.

Quinn drove around for the next thirty minutes, trying to get his head together, going over the events of the evening. What was happening to him? Up until he met Rae he'd gone through his days without feeling, without any thought other than waiting for it to end.

Since she'd marched into his life, she forced him to confront himself, his past, his present, his future. She pushed his music back in his face, brought him to the studio, invited him to clubs—compelled him to interact with the world again. All the things he'd stopped caring about.

Jamel, Rae, Max, Mrs. Finch . . . and now that old woman—they were all swarming around him, buzzing, buzzing in his head, stirring up buried thoughts, making him feel. Damn, it was so much easier not to. He pulled to a stop and realized he was back in front of Rae's building. Fate? He almost smiled. From the moment he met this woman, she had him doing stuff he had no intention of doing.

He looked up at her window. The lights were still on. He cut the engine and hoped she'd listen to what he had to say, would try to explain.

Rae stepped from the tub and wrapped herself in her favorite sea-green terry cloth robe, a gift from Gail last Christmas. Christmas, she mused, rubbing body oil into her still damp skin. It would be here in a matter of weeks. A time for family and friends, being with the ones you loved. The holiday season had been one of sadness for her since Sterling and Akia. Generally, she locked herself in the house and didn't take calls until after the New Year. She didn't want to hear the holiday greetings, have to decline the ceaseless stream of party invitations because she wasn't up to the joy that everyone else shared that she could no longer feel, see families shopping together, buying trees and gifts for that special someone. When she'd met Quinn during the summer, she'd secretly hoped that they could close out the year together and move into the next one. It didn't seem that that was going to happen. And she knew it was partly her fault.

She wanted it all, demanded more than she was willing to give. She wanted him to turn over his heart and soul to her, when she was only ready to come halfway. She knew she was taking the easy way out, hiding behind her demands and expectations, *her* wants. Could she really blame him for shutting her out? Quinn wasn't the kind of guy who simply lay back and gave it all. She knew that and still she pushed. Just as she did with everything else in her life, until she lost.

She didn't want to lose him. Lord knew she didn't. But this was uncharted territory, new ground. And she had no road map for Quinn, or even for herself. Somehow she had to find it, for both of their sakes.

He only hesitated for a moment before ringing the bell. Second-guessing himself at this point was useless. Either she'd listen or she wouldn't.

Rae peeked out of the window, sure that someone was ringing the wrong buzzer. If she'd been asleep, she'd really be pissed off. It was nearly two A.M. The last person she expected to see was Quinn, standing on her steps. Well, she asked for a road map, maybe this was the starting point.

She buzzed the door, silently praying that the detours wouldn't turn into roadblocks.

Rae sat on one of the floor pillows opposite Quinn, deciding that this time she would let him take the lead. She sipped on the cup of herbal tea she'd made for them both, while Quinn held his between his hands, staring into the amber brew as if it held the answers that he sought.

"I want to apologize . . . about tonight," he finally began. "There wasn't a reason for me to go off on you like that, act all crazy. And that was a lousy way to tell you about my son."

She remained quiet, letting him speak.

He shook his head sharply, his features pinched in frustration. "So much has been happening lately you know . . . to me . . . inside . . . in my head." He glanced up at her, held her gaze for a moment before looking away. "When I met you I just figured it would be 'a thing,' you know, someone to get with from time to time."

She inwardly cringed at his bluntness but held her tongue.

He shrugged his right shoulder. "Didn't turn out like that, Rae."

She tugged on her bottom lip to keep herself from talking, not wanting to cut off what he'd begun.

"It's just that it's been a while since a woman's been in my life for more than a minute." The corner of his mouth quirked upward. "I know I want you in my life, Rae, just don't know how much yet. I can't ask you to hang around until I work it out."

Slowly, Rae nodded. This was the detour she hadn't anticipated. "I see," she said softly. She rose from the pillow to sit beside him, gently tucking that stray lock behind his ear. "Maybe we fell into each other's lives at the wrong time, Quinn. You know. All the pieces are there, they just don't fit." Her voice wavered for a moment, but she continued. "I care about you, Quinn . . . more than care about you, but you're right, I can't nor will I wait forever."

"So now what?"

She got up, began to walk away, tightening the belt of her robe around her waist. "So . . . now I guess we go back to where we were before we met." She pulled in a breath and her resolve.

"Is that what you really want?"

She spun to face him. "Sometimes when it comes to you, I don't know what I want. Sometimes I just want to run as fast and as far away from you as I can." She swallowed over the knot in her throat, seeing the inevitable end drawing closer. "Other times I . . . I want to know what it's like to have the whole man, love the whole man, not just a part of him. I want to be that person in your life that matters."

"Things are so clear for you, Rae. Me . . ." he said, his voice trailing off, feeling everything suddenly slipping away, his anchor shifting. He stepped up to her and cupped her face in his palm. "I've been alone for a long time, Rae. A long time. Being with someone, meaning something to someone, living up to expectations . . . I just . . ."

She looked up at him, her heart aching for the anguish and conflict she saw reflected in his eyes. "Are you willing to at least try?"

He slid his arm around her waist, pulling her close. "It's not going to be easy, Rae."

"I know," she whispered.

His dark eyes roamed slowly over her face, asking permission, which she gave, letting her lips gently touch his.

Deep in her heart she knew she shouldn't have him this way, give herself to him this way, at this time, when they were both so vulnerable, so uncertain. But she couldn't stop the heat that raced through her body when his hands caressed her spine, her hips, cupping her to him, letting her feel the strength of his erection, his need for her.

She wanted him. It was as simple, as carnal as that. She wanted this man, wanted to love him, to heal him and maybe herself in the process.

When he slid his hands beneath the folds of her robe and stroked the tips of her nipples, her knees nearly gave way beneath her. Her soft moan, a mixture of agony and ecstasy, slid into his mouth in unison with her tongue, which did a slow, sensual dance with his.

"Rae," he whispered hot and feverish against her neck, pulling the robe down to expose her shoulders, her chest, the ample rise of her breasts. He lowered his head as she instinctively arched her back against the support of his strong embrace, taking one taut berry-colored nipple into his mouth, savoring the texture of it, relishing the warmth of her body, the feel of her satiny flesh beneath his hands.

Rae tugged the belt loose, letting it fall into a cottony pool at her feet, wanting him to see her, experience her in full. She stepped back, bold now, her desire for him evident in the almost smoky look in her eyes. She stretched her hands out to him, offering him more than just her body, a resting place for his soul, if only for one night. When he finally reached for her hands, and followed her to her bedroom, she knew that this was one of many steps they would take to cross the chasm that separated them.

Rae slowly backed toward her bed, still holding his

hands, his gaze. For a man who always appeared to be cool and in control even in the heat of revelations, for the first time she saw uncertainty in his eyes.

"Quinn?" she whispered. She saw his throat work up and down, but no words came. She crossed the short space between them, cupped his face in her hands. "It's okay," she said urgently. "No strings, no ties, just tonight, you and me." One by one she unfastened the buttons to his shirt, then pushed it off his shoulders and down his arms. She unbuckled his belt, slid down the zipper of his pants, and pushed them to his ankles. With nimble fingers she played with the band of his briefs, intermittently teasing his penis, which jumped and pulsed at her touch until she had those off as well.

She wanted to be as cool as he, but she couldn't. He was true beauty to behold. Even in the soft light of the bedroom, she could easily make out the cut of muscle in his chest and arms as if they were carved. His long, lean torso dipped to a taut stomach that rippled under her touch. Nestled in the triangular patch of thick hair, was the center of his manhood.

She almost cried out when she took him into her hand, gently massaging the smooth skin, simple camouflage for the hard muscle beneath.

Then without warning, he picked her up and took her to bed, the fire in his eyes and his escalated breathing causing her heart to race, no longer sure of what to expect.

In a breath he was braced above her, rocking his hips against her center without entering her. She thought she would go mad, until he touched her there, with merely a fingertip, tenderly teasing the bud that seemed to bloom with each caress.

Her body began to move of its own volition as he played with her, teased her, took her to new heights of pleasure. He seemed to be everywhere at once, and surely he must be, because her entire body was on fire. His tongue was like a trained masseuse, eliciting sounds of pleasure wherever it landed. But when he took her into his mouth, her body convulsed as the first wave of her climax hit her with such force that her voice echoed throughout the four-room apartment. And it wouldn't stop. Her body trembled and shuddered, her head thrashed back and forth on the now damp pillow as he held her hips securely in his hands and continued to pleasure her until she was sure she would faint.

She called his name over and over, but it was as if he didn't hear her, didn't want to hear her pleas. And just when she was certain she could endure no more he raised up, sliding a condom along his length, the momentary halting of pleasure nearly sending her over the edge with longing. And then, the length and breadth of him filled her in one deep thrust, taking her breath away.

He moved slow and easy, the way he walked. Took his time with her until she'd adjusted her body to his, matched his movements, caught her breath. And little by little the pace quickened, the push and pull into her body became more urgent, more demanding. His low groans hummed in her ears, until he raised up, pulling her hips to match him stroke for stroke until the grip and release of her sex was more than he could take and the shuddering climax tore through him with a power, yet a serenity he'd never before known.

When he lay with her, nestled in his arms, listening

to the beat of her heart, he thought about what had happened between them, how he'd felt, how it frightened him with its intensity. He knew that this was no one-night stand, no matter what she'd said.

Chapter Fifteen

Rae arose with the sun. Though she felt as if she could remain forever curled beside Quinn, her swirling thoughts pushed her from the bed. She sat in the neat kitchen sipping an early morning cup of tea.

There was no doubt that what happened between her and Quinn was no less than mind altering. Her body was still buzzing and humming from their lovemaking, the ache between her thighs a clear indicator that it was no dream. But something else had happened as well. Something she hadn't banked on. For all her pronouncements about no ties, no promises, she knew in her heart of hearts that's what she'd wanted. She'd taken a big gamble. And now, as she sat there she wasn't sure if Quinn made love with her because she gave him that easy option, or because he truly cared about her, at least half as much as she cared about him.

Now, not only did she have their relationship to consider, however it turned out, but the reality of his relationship with this Maxine, the mother of his son. He'd been real curt about it, almost matter-of-fact, and that more than anything put her on notice. It wasn't as cut and dried as he'd pretended. Even in the dimly lit club, she could see that look of longing, possibly regret in his eyes.

"Hey, I didn't hear you get up."

Rae turned on the stool. "Hi. Couldn't sleep." She scanned his face for a sign, any sign that last night meant as much to him as it did to her. She couldn't read him. "Want some tea?"

He smiled and her heart, as always, stirred.

"Yeah, that would be cool."

Rae made a move to get up.

"Naw, stay put. I can get it." He fixed a cup of tea and settled on the stool opposite her. "So what's on your mind, Rae? And no bull, awright?"

For a moment she was taken aback by his directness. Quinn was usually the one to skirt an issue for as long as possible, unless you nailed him to the wall. She swallowed a sip of tea and tried to collect her thoughts.

"Well . . . um . . . I know this sounds like a cliché, but about last night . . ."

He chuckled and the knot in her chest eased somewhat.

"Yeah." He angled his head to the side. "What about last night, baby?"

When he looked at her like that it was hard to keep her thoughts in order, say what was really on her mind. She looked away, regaining her balance. "I, um, meant what I said about no ties, no pressure. So I don't want you to think that I'm going to be on you like glue because we . . .''

''Made love, Rae,'' he supplied.

She nodded briskly.

''I see. So it's cool if things just stay the way they are?'' He rose from his seat, slowly moving toward her. ''What happened with us was just a thing, no big deal, right?''

He was up on her now and she couldn't breathe. She needed to get away, but she couldn't seem to move.

''Look me in the eye, Rae, and tell me it didn't mean nothin' and I'm out, okay. No hard feelin's, no regrets.'' He tipped her chin with his palm. ''Tell me.''

''I . . . it . . .''

''Tell me, Rae. I need to hear the words. I need you to tell me that my loving you last night didn't mean anything to you.'' His gaze bore into her, challenging her.

''Damn you, Quinn!'' She tugged away and he let her go. Wrapping her arms around her body she walked into the living room and sat down on one of the pillows, breathing heavily.

Quinn appeared in the doorway. Tenuously, she looked up at him. Why was it so hard for her to say what was in her heart, what was on her mind? Maybe it was because she knew the power of words. They could live with you long after the moment is gone. And once they were said, there was no taking them back. If she lived in her mind, holding on to that last piece of herself, she couldn't have regrets, wouldn't have to take things back, wish she hadn't said them, be condemned by them, measured by them. But if she didn't speak them, at this moment, she knew that something more would be lost. And she would be no different than the person Quinn was evolving from, the one she'd insisted that he let go.

"No," she said quietly. "It . . . wasn't just a thing. Not for me." She swallowed. "I lied." She smiled weakly when she saw his expression soften to one of relief.

"Lied? I'm surprised at you, Rae," he teased, moving toward her. "Not a nice quality. But I'm sure you had a good reason, right?" He reached for her hands and pulled her to her feet. "Wanna tell me what it is?" he said quietly.

"Tell me about Maxine," she said, shifting the weight from her to him, a momentary way out.

"Is that why you said what you did, because of Max?" he asked. "You're worried about Max?"

"She is your son's mother. She must have meant something to you."

"Once upon a time," he countered, his unresolved issues with Maxine and his son still raw.

"Did you love her?"

His eyes darkened. "What is this about, some relationship I had years ago?" he tossed back, his tone growing edgy.

"It's not just *some* relationship, Quinn, and you know it. If it was, you wouldn't be so bent out of shape. She must have meant something to you. She's raising your son."

That hit his last nerve. "Yeah, she and Taylor, the happy couple, are raising *my* son! Happy now, that what you wanted to hear? Did you also want to hear that she never told me about him until he was three years old?'' His voice cracked, as he stood stock-still, his body vibrating with pent-up rage. ''Came to Nikita's funeral to tell me about Jamel. What kinda shit is that, huh? You got the answers to everything. Tell me.''

''Quinn . . . I didn't . . .''

''You didn't what, Rae? Didn't think it would bother Quinn, huh? Just figured you'd back him into a corner again. Get the goods on him and run, right?''

''Quinn—''

''Save it, Rae. You were right. It's best no strings, no promises.'' He stalked across the room, snatched his coat from the hook on the wall, and slammed out.

''Rae, stop crying and tell me what happened,'' Gail insisted, trying to make sense of what her friend was saying between her rambling and her tears. ''You got me over here, now tell me what's going on, girl.''

''I really blew it, Gail.'' Rae sniffled loudly, and curled up on her bed, still rumpled from her session with Quinn.

Gail took a quick look around, saw what she assumed was Quinn's discarded shirt still in a heap on the floor. The scent of sex lightly lingered in the air. Gail's mind shifted into sinister.

''Did he hurt you? 'Cause if he hurt you—''

''No. No,'' Rae mumbled, shaking her head. ''It wasn't him . . . it was me . . . being a witch.''

Gail frowned. ''Rae, I swear if you don't explain

yourself, *I'm* gonna hurt you. Start from the beginning."

Rae snatched a tissue from the box on her night table and wiped her eyes. Finally she sat up and painfully began to unfold the events of the previous evening; from the club, to his departure, leaving nothing out.

Chapter Sixteen

"Sometimes you have to not listen to your body, because it'll lie to you," Gail said matter-of-factly. "I can't count the times I've slept with guys, then wondered what the hell I was doing. You have to slow things down so you can see the whole picture before you jump off and do something stupid. You know what I mean, girl?"

Rae wiped her eyes with a tissue, then blew her nose. "Well, it's too late for that now. Where were you when I needed you to talk some sense into my head?"

"Yeah, the damage is done now," Gail said, sitting on the edge off the bed. "But what's next?"

"I don't really know," Rae said, tossing one of the pillows into a chair. "I think I screwed up. Maybe I was too easy. Who knows what he thinks of me now."

Gail grabbed one of the blankets, folded it over,

and put it on the chair with the pillow. "It's too late to second-guess about giving him your body. The thing that worries me is your reasoning, why you gave it up like that. Do you love him? That's the real question here."

Yes, that was the real question. Did she love him? Or was it something else? Maybe she'd just wanted to get her swerve on, get laid. If it was that, then she had to be honest with herself and not play mind games. Hell, she didn't know where she stood with him. He was so in a funk, it could have just been physical release for him. No strings, no commitment—isn't that what she'd said? Still, if that was the case, why was she pissed about it? And then there was this other chick, Maxine, and the child. That was definitely something she hadn't figured on.

"I think I love him, Gail," she said. "But he's got a load of baggage. A dead wife, another woman and a kid. Man, if I had good sense, I'd run like hell away from him. But I can't. Something in me wants me to stick, to play it out to the end."

Gail pulled the end of the sheet up from the mattress. "Did they have any kids?" she asked, wondering what other skeletons were in the closet.

Rae sighed long and deep, and tugged at the sheet from her end. "No kids, thank God. They weren't married long. But he still hasn't gotten over her—what happened. I think he was really in love with her. I don't know what he feels about his son's mother. That worries me."

"Talk about complications. How old is the child?"

"I guess he's pretty young. Quinn hasn't filled in all of the details for me, so I'm in the dark about most of it. So of course my mind is working overtime.

I'm sure he'll tell me, at some point,'' she said, not really sure at all.

''You need to know the whole story before you go any further into it. But hey, it might not be as bad as you think. If they live on the West Coast, at least they're not all up in your face. You can deal with that. There is no magic formula to love. It comes in the strangest packages. You remember my thing with Edwin?''

''Sure, that was a trip,'' Rae said, placing the folded sheet on top of the blanket.

''And he had a kid he was raising, Zachary,'' Gail said, grinning widely. ''We had a ball for quite a while, until his job sent him down South. He was one hot brother, had everything a woman could want. But I understood why he took the transfer, to make more money for the boy. I still think about him sometimes.''

''Yeah, and you guys were great,'' Rae said. ''I really liked you together. Do you still hear from him?'' She asked, relieved for a moment to take the spotlight off her.

''All the time. He sends me letters, pictures of the boy, news about what he's doing. The one thing he never says in his letters is that we'll get back together and I dig that because at least he's honest. I hate dudes that lie all the time. Edwin never did that.''

''I don't know if I can be friends with Quinn, if things don't work out,'' Rae said. ''He's so volatile, on edge. Raw. He needs so much and I don't know if I'm the one to give him what he needs.''

''Then why do you think it's even worth it?'' Gail asked, always one to get to the crux of everything.

Rae sighed. ''Because underneath all of the bluster, the macho jive, there's a really beautiful man there, with so much going for him,'' Rae replied, reaching into the cabinet for fresh linen. ''I don't think he even knows how much he has going for him.''

''That's all well and good, but you don't want to get into a rescue mission, because that has nothing to do with love,'' Gail said sternly. ''I've done that, trying to change guys, save them from themselves, and that never works. He has to want to change. In the end, too much rescue work can eat away at whatever love you have for him. It'll kill it dead. Rae, be honest. Is he too injured emotionally for you to get into a real relationship with?''

''Yes, Quinn's messed up right now. But I think that's only because he's trying to deal with a lot of changes and challenges in his life. The pain he's feeling now is from growing. It ain't easy to throw out old stuff that's deep down in your soul. And that's what he's trying to do. He wants to grow and change. Just like me.''

''Are you sure of that, Miss Girl?''

Rae slipped on a pillowcase and looked over her shoulder. ''Yeah, I'm sure.''

''Cool. About these arguments, you've got to get to the point where you recognize each other's differences, allow room for that,'' Gail counseled. ''Don't try to make yourselves into duplicates of each other. That's fatal. Listen to what each other has to say. If things are too heated to do that, take a time-out, get a drink of water, go to the bathroom, or out for a walk. Cool down before you get back into it. If you're in a relationship, winning shouldn't be the big thing. Working things out is more important than scoring points. Edwin taught me that. Before I met him, I had to win. I lost two guys like that, running my mouth and not knowing when to shut up."

"When did you get so wise?" Rae said, laughing.

"When I stopped thinking like a teenybopper and started acting my age," her friend said. "As long as you know you want to be with him, hang tough, be yourself, and let things flow. Don't try to force anything. You can't make him love you. He has to come to that decision for himself. He could love you and not even know it. That happens a lot with men. They're not as in touch with their hearts as we are."

"What about this other woman, this Maxine?"

"Rae, there's not much you can do there," Gail said, shrugging, tucking one end of the sheet under the mattress. "You let him tell you what's going on there. You get all of the facts, then you make up your mind. But don't jump the gun. Wait. If it's just about his child, about how he misses him and all that, that shouldn't stop you from getting with him. Hey, be thankful that he cares like that about his kid. A lot of brothers don't."

"Hey, I know that," Rae said, smiling. "Yeah, Quinn's a good man."

"Well, that's settled," Gail said, tossing a pillow at her friend. "Now go get him, tiger. Never let a good man slip through your fingers. They don't grow on trees. What time is it?"

"A little after one." She threw a pillow back at Gail but the woman ducked and laughed at her.

"Rae, I've got to get out of here," her friend said, walking toward the door. "Called the dentist yesterday. Got two back teeth that need work. I hope he doesn't have to use the drill. Hate that thing. Or worse yet, have to pull them, hours in that chair.

Anyway, see ya, honey. Got to run. Stick it out with Quinn. He sounds all right. Give him a shot. You deserve to be happy."

After Gail left, Rae stared at the pile of soiled linen, the evidence of her torrid night with Quinn. She walked over, grabbed the sheet that was ripe with the aroma of their love, husky and carnal, and sat on the bed. Without a second thought, her hands brought it up to her nose and she inhaled deeply as though she were going underwater.

For some reason, Quinn stopped at the door of B.J.'s, watching the group of black men sitting and squatting on the cars a half block down from the bar, shooting dice. They were having a friendly game of craps, no arguing, no scrapping. He smiled and nodded before pushing open the old Plexiglas door. As usual, Turk was behind the bar, serving a few early afternoon regulars some brews. Other guys lined the long wood glancing up at the Saints-Vikings football game, bickering about which NFL teams would make the playoffs, which quarterback had the strongest arm, and which defense unit gave up the least scores. Turk paid them no mind. He perked up when he saw Quinn walk in.

"Whassup, stranger?" the bartender asked, all smiles. "What you been up to?"

"Nothing much," Quinn answered, looking around. "All's cool."

"You lookin' for Remy? He's in the back, getting his gear together. Today's his fishing day, out on that rickety boat of his. He loves that piece of crap, thinks he's Captain Ahab or somethin'. Go on back, kid."

"Thanks, man."

The back room was still small, a little larger than a cell in lockup, and just as rank smelling as usual. Sweat, booze, bodies, perfume, you name it. Nobody remembered to put in a stronger lightbulb, so the glow in the room was faint, eerie, almost otherworldly. Quinn squinted his eyes, trying to make out the faces of the handful of people gathered near a battered pool table in a corner of the room. At least the pictures of the women on the walls had been changed. Remy, ever the mack, loved a pretty woman. Out of the shadows, Smalls, the ever faithful bouncer, waddled over to Quinn, about to frisk him, when a familiar raspy voice cut through the cigarette fog.

"Leave the man alone," Remy said, appearing out of the crowd, holding a fishing pole. "Come on over, kid, and let me check ya out."

Quinn and the older man hugged as men do, patting each other on the back. They remained that way for three seconds until Remy, dressed in casual fishing gear, stepped back. He looked at his young protégé long and hard, nodding his head in approval.

"Look good, my man," the slickster said in a grumble. "Whatcha been doing since I seed ya last?"

Quinn noticed the once salt-and-pepper hair was now more salt than pepper. The years were passing. He smiled, his heart warm at the sight of the old man. "Hey, I'm hanging, doing my thing. Everything's pretty decent but I would like some words with you, Mr. R."

"No problem. Had some business I had to wrap up with my man over there. You remember Willie Stiles, once was the big man around here. All through Harlem, even up in the Bronx. Ran girls, numbers, a couple of after-hour clubs, hot sheet hotels, had his hand in everything. Well, one of his girls turned up dead. They pinned the rap on Willie, did a long stretch up in Sing Sing. Just got out. Willie, come over here. Wantcha to meet somebody.''

Willie looked older than Remy, had the stoop of somebody who'd been inside a long time, thin and gaunt. His face was like that of an eagle, all angles and corners. He was dressed all in black, turtleneck and pants, long coat and cowboy boots. Shades hid his eyes and an old-style stingy brim covered his head. Anyone could see that Remy had much respect for the old school gangster by the way he deferred to him.

''Glad to meet you, youngblood,'' Willie said, his lips barely moving. ''Remy, we can conversate on that other thing later this evening. Call me when you get back from the water.''

He shook Quinn's hand, the diamond ring on his pinkie throwing off rays, then he was gone. Remy started talking to Quinn about how the numbers game wasn't what it used to be, with the lotto and all, how the young thugs were muscling in on a lot of the other hustles, how heroin, or ''boy'' as he called it, was making a comeback. He talked as he gathered up his fishing gear, the rods, the box with his lures and bait.

Once outside, they walked to his new ride, a brand-new Jaguar, two-door. Fire-engine red. Quinn could tell he was proud of the car by the way he patted it before opening the door on the driver's side. ''Hop in. We can talk while we ride,'' Remy instructed. They pulled away from the curb, cruising slowly.

''Quinn, guess what?'' He turned west, going toward the river.

"What?" He loved watching the old man, his style, his sense of cool. They didn't make black men like him anymore, strong, polished, and solid.

"Man, I'd love to go down to the Keys one day and fish for marlin and swordfish," Remy said, his eyes sparkling. "I love this fishing thing. Relaxes you. You get on the water, throw your line in, and the world just drifts away. You need to get back out here to cool you right out."

Quinn remembered once going with his "Uncle" Ike and his crew fishing off Long Island, the men wrestling with the big ones, and the rows of long gray fish strung along the block and tackle, their insides removed and fins cut off. Ike drank, smoked his cigars, and bragged about the ones that got away. They had a good time. It was one of the first times he recalled feeling like a man, a real man, hanging out with the old guys. Chilling.

They parked the car near the water, locked it up, and walked over to the pier. Remy pointed out his boat, a not-so-small fishing craft with an outboard motor on the back. It had sleeping quarters, a galley, a TV, and a modern guidance system. The old man got him onboard and cast off, heading out to sea. They didn't say much until he got out beyond the harbor into the open water. He offered Quinn a cold beer and the two men sat for awhile, catching up on old times.

"How you doin'? You okay?"

Quinn noticed the boats out on the horizon, some fishing, others carrying cargo. "Yeah, I'm dealing. But I've got a bunch of other stuff gnawing at me, Remy. My life's all messed up. I got a son I never see, you know the deal with that. Still can't play. Haven't written a word for my book that's overdue, and now I've got this new woman who wants to get close to me. Sometimes I don't know if I'm coming or going."

"Hmmm," was all Remy said, as if that was enough. And for the moment it was. All Quinn wanted right then was some peace and a willing ear, no accusations, no judgments.

There was a stiff land breeze from Remy's right. He moved the gear and box to the middle of the deck, watching the water, its eddies and currents moving in a steady dark stream. Quinn was glad that he had come. The serenity of the sea took his mind off his problems for a while but he knew he had to talk with the old man, get it out, settle the confusion. Overhead, a group of large gulls sailed, glided, then dived into the water after food.

"You can eat the fish from out here, but I wouldn't cook any of the fish caught from the Hudson," Remy said, attaching bait to his line. "The water over there is so polluted, even the fish look sick."

Cooking. Quinn remembered in a flash Nikita's slender body standing next to his in the kitchen of their apartment, her fingers clumsily trying to bread some strip of whiting, the coating all over the place. When she dropped the strip, she turned to him and gave him her famous half smile. Even now, he could see her glorious body, recall how she looked so delicious in clothes, no matter what she wore. Oh how those T-shirts clung to her! But she couldn't cook to save her life. She was a total disaster in the kitchen.

"What's on your mind, son?" Remy asked, preparing to cast a line into the water.

"Mr. R, I'm all screwed up in the head," Quinn said, watching the slow churning of the blades in the water. "I think I've come through the grieving thing over Niki, worked through that for the most part, but now there's a new woman in my life. She wants to get into something. I don't know if I'm ready. I still feel raw inside. All of this old stuff I've got to work through. It's like life doesn't let you stop and take a deep breath. Everything's always coming at you."

"Do you like this new woman?" Remy asked, looking up at the gray clouds far off. "You notice I said nothing about love. I don't trust that love at first sight crap. You like her, the new one?"

"Yeah, she's stable and consistent, talented," Quinn said. "A solid sistah."

"Does she keep you in check?" Remy had two poles now over the water.

"That's just it. We've been going at it back and forth. She's always deep in my stuff, probing, digging, won't let me get off with some jive answer. She's tough. Niki used to do that. But it's different with Rae."

Remy laughed. "I once knew a woman named Rae. She was a wild, crazy girl. Party girl but down-to-earth. The real article. Rae-Rae, we called her. Now your Rae, how much you know about her?"

Quinn stood, feeling the breeze on his face, his eyes riveted on the old man walking briskly from the bait box to one of the poles at the rail of the boat. Its line was now taut, straining under the weight of the fish's pull. Remy calmly gripped the rod in one hand, started reeling the fighting fish in, yanking it back easily. The water rippled, its surface disturbed by the conflict; then the long back of the gray fish became visible. With a quick jerk of his arm, he swung it over the side and onto the deck.

"Get that big bucket with the lid on it," Remy ordered.

Quinn brought the bucket and watched as his mentor separated the struggling fish from the hook, its mouth agape. "Man, it's big!"

Looking up from his kneeling position near the bucket, Remy smiled, then asked again, "So how much do you know about the girl, the new one?"

"She has her stuff like anybody but none of it is the kind of craziness that would scare me off. I think we could have something if we just settled down."

"Good." Remy put the rod back in the water, looked up at the sky. "Winter's coming. Real winter coming soon. No more of these fake spring days. Anyway, that's good. If she's a decent girl, give the thing time. It's like fishing. The fun part is the wait. You have to have patience, give the fish time to decide what to do. You can't rush him. If you do, you'll chase him off. That's what you need in this, patience, give it time, and what will be will be."

"What about Max and Jamel?" Quinn asked, concern on his face. "I don't know how she'll react to all that. You know how women are. Another woman and a child. They head for the hills."

"Not if she's worth anything," Remy said. "Hell, she's grown. She knows you had a life before you met her. She'll deal with it if she cares about you. You take somebody into your life, you take everything that comes with them. Don't worry about it."

The rod shook, another fish on the hook. This time Remy turned to Quinn and said, "You take him in, son." Quinn went over and did as he had seen the old man do. Struggling, he started reeling it in, the fish not as big as the other, but putting up a good fight. After he landed it, Remy patted him on the shoulder much as a proud father would do and broke out some food. Sandwiches, chips, and a couple of cold brews. They sat in silence, watching the lines, the other boats, the dark clouds, and felt at peace with the water and themselves.

Later that day, Quinn sat in his living room, listening to Roy Hargrove on trumpet and Johnny Griffin on tenor play sweetly on the ballad *"When We Were One,"* their soft, silky sounds filling the space. It had been a cool day. Real nice spending time with Mr. R. He was the closest thing Quinn had ever had to a father. He drank his Jack Daniels on the rocks and thought about everything Remy had told him. *Patience.* Let everything take its time. He closed his eyes, sank into the warm arms of the music, its serenity, its gentle sway like the movement of the boat that day. Then the doorbell rang. Grumbling, he got up, put down his drink, and walked over to open it.

It was Rae.

"I know what I want, Quinn," she said without preamble, staring him down in the doorway. "I'm not going to give you up this easy and walk away. Do you want to be with me or not?" Her heart thundered in her chest as forever seemed to tick by.

Slowly his eyes roamed across her face, down the length of her body. He leaned down and tenderly kissed her lips. "I was going to ask you the same thing," he whispered, before pulling her inside and kicking the door shut behind them.

Chapter Seventeen

This relationship thing wasn't too bad, Quinn mused, watching Rae putter around in her kitchen. Since they'd come to terms that they really wanted to be a couple, really work things out, it wasn't as difficult or as intrusive as he'd imagined.

He liked the idea of waking up with Rae, hearing her hum in the shower, walking up behind him and kissing him in the ear, asking him what he was thinking. Most times he would tell her, and most times she would tell him when he asked. And it was all good.

He was beginning to understand her because he'd slowly begun to realize that they were very much alike in many ways, and, yeah, it was going to take some time to knock all the kinks out, but as Remy said, he had to learn patience.

"Looks like it's gonna snow," Rae commented, peering out of the kitchen window.

"You mind if I hide out over here for a while?" he asked. " 'Cause I know with the first flake, Mrs. Finch is gonna have me shoveling and salting like we're in the middle of a blizzard."

Rae laughed. "Be nice. That woman loves you to death. She just keeps you busy because it makes her feel good by keeping you out of trouble."

"Yeah," he said with a sarcastic chuckle. "That's the line she keeps running on me."

Rae came up to him and plopped down on his lap, wrapping her arms around his neck. "It's true, baby," she cooed. "If she didn't have you running all over the place, just think of all the mischief you could get yourself into." She kissed him on the lips. "Know what I mean?" she said in a sultry whisper, sliding her hand under his shirt.

"Oh, you mean this kind of trouble." He cupped her breast until she moaned in pleasure, and nuzzled her neck.

"Yeah . . . this kind of trouble."

Satisfied from a draining session of lovemaking, Rae had no intention of moving from her very comfortable position next to Quinn, wrapped up in her down quilt and watching the first flakes of snow fall beyond her window.

This is what she'd been hoping for, she thought dreamily, to be in a relationship on equal footing. Although Quinn still steered clear of the studio, he was at least contemplating playing again. At least it was something he was considering. That was definitely a good sign.

Both of them were moving forward, taking steps but instead of walking that path alone, they were doing it together. She'd finally told him the full story about her and Sterling, that their issues were never about his parents, but her, her drive, something Sterling could never quite understand. Yes, there would always be sorrow, sorrow for the husband she lost and mostly for the child that she would never see grow up. It was the kind of pain she still couldn't put into words, and Quinn seemed to understand that.

In a way she envied the fact that he had a son, a child that he could pick up a phone and talk to, hear his laughter and all the funny stories that children tell. See his face, watch him change. She sighed deeply. If there was one thing she'd come to realize, you couldn't change the past, only learn from your mistakes and move on. That was a part of her life that was gone. Now, instead of allowing the memories to weigh her down, she would use them to spur her on.

She snuggled closer to him and he stirred.

"Don't move," he mumbled. "You feel too good right where you are."

"You might just have to stay put for real. The snow is here."

Quinn groaned.

Rae giggled and nudged him in the side. "As much as I hate to see you go, you know Mrs. Finch is going to be frantic."

He groaned again.

"Come on, you big baby. I'll get dressed and come with you. How's that?"

Slowly he sat up, reached for her, and kissed her slow and long. "Sounds like a real incentive to me."

After shoveling the inch-high dusting of snow and salting down the front walk and the steps to Mrs. Finch's precise instructions, Quinn tiptoed upstairs hoping she wouldn't hear him.

When he returned, Rae was reclining on the couch reading a magazine and listening to some music. She looked up. "All done?"

"Yeah, and if you cared about me like you claim you do, you'd offer to give a tired brother a massage for all the hard work he's done."

Rae grabbed a pillow from behind her head and threw it at him, catching him on the shoulder.

"See, that's what I mean. If I wasn't so tired, I could have ducked. Between you and Mrs. Finch you try to wear a brother out."

"Consider yourself lucky. Some men would love to be in your place."

"Sure, having two women mistreat him. Yeah, I bet they're standing in line for that."

He came and sat down beside her. "What are you reading?"

"Sears catalog. Just looking at some stuff for Christmas. They say they can have it here by Christmas if I order in the next two days. Kinda iffy to me, though," she said, picking up the catalog and flipping through the pages. "With Christmas just about two weeks away . . ."

Quinn stood. "Yeah, uh, I wanted to talk to you about that."

Her radar immediately went up by his tone. She

put the catalog down and gave him her full attention. "What's up?" she asked as casually as she could.

"Uh, Jamel is coming down for the holidays, spending some time with me."

Her pulse rate slowly returned to normal. Jamel, fine, no big deal. She needed to get to know him anyway. "That's great, Quinn. It'll be fun, we'll plan some stuff, take him around the city, maybe—"

"Maxine is coming too," he said, cutting to the chase. "She's going to stay with her folks." He walked over to the CD player and changed the disk to Chaka Khan's "Epiphany."

"Uh-huh, and . . . what is it that you're not telling me?"

"Her husband can't get away until Christmas Eve. It's just her and J, and she wants me to pick them up from the airport. She was talking about us spending some time together . . . you know, me, her, and J, but . . ." He shook his head. "I don't think that's such a cool idea."

Rae was quiet for a moment, trying to process the information, read between the lines and the expression on Quinn's face. *Maxine.* The only person she feared other than his memory of Nikita. But Maxine was flesh and blood, flesh that he'd touched, made love to, made a baby with. That was the kind of hold that could never be broken. Sure, he'd explained about Maxine, their friendship since childhood, her loyalty, and their love affair, his feelings of betrayal for what she'd done. He insisted he was over her. But there was a part of Rae that wondered if that would ever be true. And if not, where would that leave her?

"So where do I fit in during this lovefest?" she asked a bit more nastily than she intended.

Quinn came over to her, sat beside her, and put his arm around her shoulder, drawing her close. "Listen to me." He looked into her eyes and saw the fear in them. "You'll be with me," he said tenderly. "Every step of the way." He held her close, cradling her head against his chest. "Every step, baby," he repeated. He was going to need her, more than she knew, more than he was willing to admit.

Rae'd been on pins and needles all week long. She'd completely dismantled her closet looking for the perfect outfit. She worried herself sleepless over what this Maxine looked like, what she would say to her, how Quinn and Maxine would act when they saw each other, and most of all if she would feel like the fifth wheel. Finally the day arrived.

"Would you relax, Rae," Gail admonished, worn out from the parade of outfits and changes in lipstick color.

Rae spun around, her hands on her hips. "Relax! How do you expect me to relax, Gail? This isn't some high school sweetheart. This is a woman he's known all his life, turned to in crises, lived with, had a child with, for heaven's sake. This is the same woman he went to when he left Nikita, the very same woman that Nikita felt threatened by even though he married her. So tell me something else. Just don't tell me to relax. Okay!"

Gail twisted her full lips, swinging her crossed leg. "Have you ever asked him why they didn't work out? Why she is happily married to someone else?"

For a moment, Rae slowed down. She tugged in a breath, then looked at Gail imploringly, wanted her to understand the depth of her angst. "It's just that we've come so far, me and Quinn. And we still have a way to go to make this thing solid. I just don't want anything to mess that up, you know?"

"Yeah, hon, I know. But Quinn is with you. Not Maxine. Yes, she has his son and there's nothing you can do about it, but deal. So you can either let her get the upper hand by allowing her to have this unseen power over you, or you can be the dynamite woman that you are, and show Quinn exactly why he's with you—and show her, too, while you're at it."

Rae lowered her eyes and bit back a smile. "You know I hate it when you're right."

"Get over it." She stood. "I have to run. Have tons of shopping still to do." She took a last look around as she slipped on her suede jacket. "I like what you did with the place," she said, noting the small, decorated tree. She turned to Rae and smiled in understanding, knowing that was a big step for her, something as simple as a tree.

"Thanks," Rae said.

Gail kissed Rae's cheek as she opened the door. "When are you back in the studio?"

"After the new year. We're all burned out, and I'm still not satisfied with the last two pieces."

Gail smiled and shook her head. "Call me if you need me."

"I will."

"And, Rae, if you believe you're worth it, so will he."

Rae was coiled as tight as a bedspring on the ride to the airport. Every now and then she'd glance at

Quinn, try to read him. His expression was impassive, as if going to the airport to meet his former lover, with his current woman, were something he did all the time.

She folded her arms. Couldn't he even ask her if she was all right? All he'd said since he came to pick her up was that she looked real good. *Big thank-you.* What she needed to hear was that he loved her, only her. That Maxine meant nothing to him, and could never come between them. All the things he'd never said, and that is what scared her.

It took all he had to concentrate on driving and not miss his exits. He had no idea how to handle something like this. He hadn't told Maxine that he was bringing Rae. He should have so that Max could have prepared J. The situation was bad enough without confusing Jamel any more with another addition to the mix. What was he thinking? That was just it, he wasn't thinking. And you'd think Rae would be a little more concerned. She couldn't possibly think this was easy for him. Not once did she ask if he was all right. Hey, fine, he'd get through it. He turned to glance at her. Her face was smooth and relaxed. *Women.*

Rae knew her the minute she stepped off the plane, and it wasn't because of the little boy whose hand she held that looked so much like his father. It was the cool class about her, the way she walked with assurance, a worldliness. She was quite stunning to look at with her dark brown features and severe haircut that accentuated her sharp cheekbones and engaging eyes. And even clothed beneath her designer attire, she had a figure that men lusted after.

Surprising Rae, Quinn took her hand, turned to her, and said, "Here they come. You cool?"

She nodded, suddenly feeling a wave of relief. She squeezed his hand. "You?"

"Yeah, no doubt."

The instant Jamel spotted his father, he was off and running. "Daaaaddy!"

Quinn swooped him up into his arms, hugging him, realizing with a pang in his chest how terribly he'd missed him, how much he loved him.

Rae watched the exchange of love with a mixture of happiness for her man, and sadness for herself. Briefly she shut her eyes, conjuring up a picture of Akia, trying to recall her scent, the lilt of her laughter. Yes, all the memories were still intact. She opened her eyes as Maxine approached. She stiffened and watched. The next few minutes were sure to tell her everything she wanted to know—or not.

"Hey, Q."

She had the kind of voice that had that just-finished-making-love sound, soft and hot, Rae observed. And she called him "Q." *She* never called him Q.

Maxine reached up and stroked Quinn's cheek, for the moment seeing only him. "You look great, Q."

And at that instant, Rae felt locked out, nowhere in the picture of the happy reunited family.

Quinn stepped back, still holding Jamel. "Max, this is my lady, Rae Lindsay. Rae, this is Maxine Sherman . . . I mean Collins." He put his free hand around Rae's waist as if to assure her that everything was okay, that Maxine had not just rocked his world.

For the first time, Maxine took full notice of Rae

Lindsay, *his lady*. She was attractive, in an understated sort of way, nothing flashy. They looked good together, she inwardly admitted, and it was clear in Quinn's protectiveness of her that she meant something to him.

The old pang of jealousy reared its ugly head, but she pushed it back down. There would always be a part of her that wondered what it was about her that couldn't hold Quinn, that always sent him into the arms of someone else. But the rational side of her knew that it had nothing to do with her, but the kind of man that Quinn was and what he needed in his life. The truth of it was, he was no longer the kind of man she needed and had not been in a long time. But there would always be those feelings of the familiar that she would keep close to her heart, the special thing that they did have between them. And because deep in her heart she would always have a love for him, she could only wish him the best, some semblance of happiness. Hopefully, Rae was the one. Funny, though, he hadn't mentioned her at all. And if she was going to be in Quinn's life, and therefore, their son's life, she wanted to know everything she could about "his lady."

Maxine stuck out her hand, pushed a smile across her lips. "Nice to meet you, Rae."

Rae took her hand. "You too. I've heard a lot about you. You . . . have a beautiful son," she added.

"Thanks."

"We better go get your bags," Quinn interjected. "You going straight to your mom's or what?"

"You know how lousy airplane food can be. We're both starved." She patted her son's head, who was still nestled in Quinn's arm. "I was thinking maybe we could stop somewhere and get something to eat."

Quinn looked at Rae.

"Sounds like a great idea," Rae offered first. "I'm kind of hungry myself." She saw the relief wash over Quinn's face. "What do you have a taste for?"

Maxine grinned. "At this point, anything."

"How 'bout Spoonbread's up on 135th?" Quinn asked. "It's not too far from your mom's and the food is great. A little small, but good service."

"Fine with me."

The midday crowd at the neighborhood soul food restaurant was minimal. The quartet was quickly seated and eagerly scanned the menu. The aroma of collard greens, barbecue ribs, and peach cobbler heightened everyone's appetite.

"I want some of everything," Maxine said, with a laugh. "It's been so long since I've had some good soul food . . ."

"How long have you lived in California?" Rae quizzed.

"A little more than six years."

"It must be a culture shock to come from such a warm climate to snow."

"Sort of. But I grew up in New York. It's more of a treat for J. He's never seen snow before." She reached over and hugged her son, whose eyes were glued to the window, watching the people trudge through what was now slush.

"Can I go outside please?" Jamel asked, looking at his mother, then his father.

Quinn shrugged. "Sure. Until the food comes."

"Put your hat on, J," Maxine instructed as he

leaped from his seat and made a mad dash for the door.

Quinn was right behind him. "Be back in a few." He looked from one woman to the other and wondered how wise it was to leave them alone, but now he had no choice. He followed Jamel outside.

"So, uh, what do you do?" Rae continued with her questions.

"I own a travel agency."

"Really. Must be great owning your own business."

"It has its merits. What about you?"

"I write music and play piano."

Surprise registered on Maxine's face. "I guess you and Quinn have a lot in common, then."

"Yeah. I just wish he would play again."

Maxine nodded. "Losing Nikita really undid him. He really hasn't been the same."

"He's getting better," Rae countered quickly. "We're working on it."

Maxine studied Rae for a moment. "You're the first woman . . . he's . . . since . . ."

"I know."

"I guess he must really care about you."

"He does," Rae said with assurance.

Maxine picked up her glass of iced tea and took a thoughtful sip. As much as she didn't want to, she liked this woman. She liked her directness, her self-assurance, even if it was for her benefit. She knew good and damned well it took a special kind of woman to casually chat with her lover's ex-girlfriend and mother of his child.

"I was just thinking," Maxine said, putting down her glass. "I have tons of shopping to do in the next few days. I thought maybe we could do it together."

Rae's stomach did a slow flip. *Maxine and me. Shopping. Together. This is truly the new millennium.* "I . . . I guess."

"Great." She pulled a piece of paper from her purse and scribbled down her mother's home number and handed it to Rae. "Give me a call when you have a minute, okay?"

"Sure." Rae took the information and pushed it into her wallet. She pulled in a breath. "Are you free tomorrow?" she asked, stepping boldly into the untested waters.

"Absolutely."

"What are you two conspiring about?" Quinn asked, walking up on the close of negotiations.

"We were making plans to Christmas shop . . . together," Rae said, looking up at him.

Quinn's brows rose as he glanced from one smiling face to the other. Together? Shopping? *Women.* Go figure. But what he really would like to know was, what could they possibly have to say to each other? Then again, maybe he didn't.

Chapter Eighteen

Pulling her collar up against the bitter wind, Rae wondered why she had agreed to go shopping with this woman who had been so deeply involved with her man. Or man-to-be. She waited for several minutes until she saw the cab pull up at the curb and a head pop out the window, calling for her to get inside. Quinn stood in the doorway, watching and waiting as his little boy jumped out of the cab and raced into his father's arms. Rae looked at the two of them in a loving embrace and turned to see the expression of contentment on Maxine's face before she stepped into the cab.

"Hey, girl, how you doing today?" Maxine asked, real energy in her voice. "You ready for our Great Shopping Adventure? Quinn has Jamel for the afternoon so we can take our time . . . get to know each other. That cool with you?"

"Sure." Rae wondered how much of this enthusiasm was an act.

"Where do you want to go first?" Maxine asked. "I was thinking we could hit Bloomie's, look around, check out the prices. If we don't get anything there, then we could slide by Saks and stop afterward for lunch somewhere."

Rae nodded. She couldn't figure this woman. Was she just being nice to get her to put her guard down? Or was she for real? While Maxine chatted away about her life on the West Coast, she sat there, taking in the sights along the streets as the cab headed toward the East Side. The holiday traffic was murder, cars bumper-to-bumper on the main thoroughfares in the midtown area. It made her uneasy but Maxine seemed to take it in stride, now talking about adding a new porch to her home and possibly selling the house after the remodeling for more money and moving up to Monterey.

Finally, the cab stopped at the north entrance of the large department store on Lexington Avenue, and they got out, wading into the crowds on the sidewalk. Rae remembered how she used to come to Bloomie's with her mother to shop for the holidays, the lights, the displays, and the mob of shoppers clogging the wide aisles. She waited for a few minutes while Maxine stopped at an ATM on the first floor to load up on cash so she wouldn't tap out her credit cards. Then they sauntered along the main floor to the cosmetics department, where one Bloomingdale staffer stood spraying fragrances on the wrists of female passersby. Both women declined her offer, pressing on, glancing through the display cases at the rows of boxes of bottles and atomizers.

They went downstairs to the men's clothing department, where Maxine bought two light sweaters for her husband, commenting how cool California evenings could get. Rae considered buying something for Quinn but didn't. After her sweater purchase, Maxine suggested they go up to the children's department on the ninth floor. Here she bought an erector set for Jamel, saying how he loved building things. Who knows, maybe he'll be an engineer?

Rae was quiet, almost sullen, wondering if she'd ever have a child to buy things for. Cute dolls for a little girl. Or a set of plastic action figures for a rambunctious boy. She watched quietly as Maxine cradled her purchases under her arm, walking through the store like a general reviewing his troops. God, she seemed so confident!

When they finished there, Maxine hailed a cab for them to go to Saks, which was nine blocks always on Fifth Avenue. They got a cab, though it became quickly stalled in traffic and they ended up jumping out about three blocks away from the store.

The wind carried a brisk chill, sharp, but without the razor's edge of the gusts earlier in the day. Neither woman complained, stepping lively among the throngs meandering at the entrances of shops, restaurants, and salons. Soon they stood under the row of American flags hung over the entrance of the fashionable store, walking in with women in jewels and furs. The pair went straight to the women's collections on the second floor, inspected the goods, imagining themselves in dresses and other outfits clearly out of their price range. Still, Maxine bought a hat, a furry thing that made Rae laugh for the first time since their shopping spree began. She cracked up even more when her newfound ''girlfriend'' put the thing on her head and joked about her husband's possible reaction to it. ''Wait until he sees this!''

As they were passing the Bridal Salon on the third floor, Maxine nudged her, feeling quite giddy, and asked: ''Do you think Quinn and you will have a big wedding?''

Rae was caught completely off guard. ''We haven't gotten that far into things yet.''

''How long have you known him?''

''A few months. We haven't talked about anything serious yet. We're still feeling each other out, trying to see if we should try the whole thing any further.''

''Are you in love with him?'' Maxine bluntly asked.

''Yes, but there are complications,'' she confessed, not sure why she did. This woman didn't need to know that anything was amiss in her relationship with Quinn.

Maxine laughed knowingly. ''With Quinn, there are always complications. But you know what? I wouldn't want a man who didn't have complications. Simple guys are boring. You want somebody you can't figure out in one sitting. Do you know what I mean?''

Rae returned her smile. She was beginning to like this woman, so natural, so real, so carefree. She spoke her mind but didn't come across as a witch. It was all so easy talking to her, too easy in a way. Still, she could see why Quinn would have fallen for her. Men always liked women who weren't limited to playing some stiff role of what they thought a woman was supposed to be, what femininity was supposed to be. Maxine was the real thing.

They circled around back to the second floor, where Maxine stopped to look at golf clubs, tees, jackets, and shoes. She explained to Rae that Taylor was itching to get out on the links since he saw Tiger Woods crush his opposition in the PGA Open. Taylor, according to Maxine, had been buying and reading every golf book and magazine he could lay his hands on. He was even talking about taking Jamel with him to one of the local parks. Maxine whispered the word *men* and winked playfully.

"I'd do anything for Taylor," Maxine said, fingering the golf jackets. "He's been a rock to me in some really bad times. You don't find guys like him every day. None of that 'I'm the man' junk. We're partners in every sense of the word. I can't wait until my baby gets here."

"How does he feel about Jamel, Quinn's son?" Rae asked cattily. Tossing out a verbal stinger.

"Hey, he could have walked out as soon as he found out, but he stayed," Maxine said. "We had some words about it. It was rough for a minute there. But he stayed. Now he loves Jamel just as if he were his own child. You oughta see those two together."

"But it must be tough raising somebody else's kid."

Maxine reached for another jacket. "People do it every day. If you love somebody, you do what you have to do. Jamel loves Taylor, but he knows who his real father is. I never let him forget that fact. Quinn is his father, no matter what."

Rae picked up a pair of golf gloves, playing with the snaps at the wrist. "You ever think about sharing custody with Quinn? Letting him keep his son half the year or something like that."

"No." Maxine's eyes flashed fire. She looked Rae full in the face, ready for battle.

"Why not?"

"Because he's comfortable living where he is. I don't think Quinn is ready to be a full-time father. He's got a lot of issues to deal with before he can even think about taking on a responsibility that large. Raising children is no joke."

Rae said nothing else. This woman, she thought, could be fierce if crossed. She'd hate to see her lose her cool, get mad about something. That was probably the other reason why Quinn loved her. Quinn and Maxine were an emotional match; each just as fiery, just as intense as the other. But so was she, she'd come to realize. She gave as good as she got. She stood toe-to-toe with him, and wasn't knocked off her feet. No, she wasn't the softie she once was.

"Let's go up to eight," Maxine said, walking away from the counter. "I want to get some Godiva chocolates for my mother. She loves sweets."

On the eighth floor, Maxine saw Rae looking across the aisle at the clothing for kids, newborns, infants, and toddlers. Making a face, she touched Rae on the arm and nodded toward the candy counter. The woman behind the counter was especially nasty, offering her the smallest box of candy possible first.

"We have one that is a little larger," said the counter woman, a thin brunette with a long nose rivaling that of the Wicked Witch of the East in the Oz stories. "Possibly that would be more in your price range."

"No, let me see that one there," Maxine said, pointing to a larger box, offering a wider array of dark treats.

The counter woman frowned, toying with her collar. "Oh dear, the price on that one is rather steep. Are you sure this is the one you want? I could show you something a bit economical."

Maxine put her hands on her hips and glared at the woman. It was the "don't mess with me" pose. "I know what I want."

The counter woman turned beet red, totally flustered, and retrieved a box from a drawer. "Anything else, ma'am?" The words were said with a tone of utter disdain.

"And I'd like the box gift-wrapped if you don't mind." Maxine kept her eyes locked on the woman. Neither woman wanted to back down but Maxine had the upper hand as the customer. *Customers are always right.*

With that business finished, Maxine suggested that they walk over to Rockefeller Center, see the big tree, act like tourists, and get a bite to eat. Rae, still slightly rattled by the Saks episode, quickly agreed. Besides, her feet were starting to hurt from all of the walking and standing.

It took them under a half hour to wander over to Rockefeller Center, stopping to look at the window where Katie, Matt, and Al held court every morning for *The Today Show,* the small shops along the short strip beside the main plaza and the arcade. They stood for a while above the ice rink, watching the skaters, some beginners and others almost pros, go through paces. Some onlookers laughed at the skaters who struggled to keep their footing and fell. When they tired of that, the women walked to a nearby café and ordered salads and coffee. Maxine stopped the waiter and ordered a slice of apple pie, saying she was breaking her diet for the holiday. A few calories never hurt, she joked.

"What was Quinn like when he was growing up?"

Rae asked, eating a piece of lettuce. "You knew him back then. You grew up together."

"He was like any of the other boys around the way, maybe a little tougher, more cocky," Maxine said. "I guess I looked up to him because I knew it must have been rough on him, not having a mother. He never groused about it. He did what he had to do for him and his sister, Lacy."

"What was she like, his sister?"

"Oh man, everybody loved Lacy. She was my girl. She was totally alive, a lot of fun. Funny, she'd make you wet yourself with some of the stuff she said. She was the exact opposite of Quinn in a lot of ways. Real open and honest. Not guarded at all. It almost killed me when she died."

"It probably almost killed Quinn, too, huh?"

"Yeah, to tell the truth, I don't think he ever got over her death. They were real close. He loved his sister."

Rae sipped her coffee and watched the sadness in the woman's eyes. "What about the mother, his mother? What happened to her?"

"Nobody knows. She just left them. I think it messes with Quinn the most. I can't imagine what it must be like to grow up without a mother. Especially when she just walks off and abandons you. Much of who Quinn is comes from that fact, that she left them high and dry. Without a word. I think that's why he rarely lets people get close to him."

"What about his wife, Nikita?" Rae asked, trying to make the most of the situation, get as much information as she could, because this opportunity might not happen again any time soon.

Maxine laughed and drank from her cup. "Yum,

vanilla roast. Anyway, Niki, Ms. Uptown Girl. What was she like? In some ways, she was exactly what Quinn needed. Sometimes I didn't see it but she was. She was something else. She was an only child. Headstrong, willful, and often as sweet as she could be. I'll tell you this. She had a way of neutralizing Quinn, of blunting his anger. She could cool him right out."

"I've seen his temper," Rae said. "He can really blow up."

"He was like that with Niki, too, at the beginning, but she had his number. The girl was no pushover. She made him deal with himself and he resisted her. But eventually he came around. A lot of people, including me, underestimated her because she was so damn pretty, and that was their mistake. She was one strong, determined sistah. Quinn needed that. She didn't let him get away with nothing."

Rae went for broke. "Why did you two break up, you and Quinn?"

Maxine almost choked, coughed a few times, and drank some water. *This girl is direct, straight from the shoulder,* she thought. *She doesn't mince words. Good. That's just what Quinn needs. Not some phony stiff chick.*

"We were never together," Maxine answered. "Not like you think."

"I don't get it," Rae stuttered. "But . . . Jamel."

"That's a long story. Not one I really want to get into right now."

"But weren't you two . . . together at some point?"

"Yeah, we had a thing. But I think we both knew it wouldn't last. It was something that evolved out of need and familiarity, I think. I don't know what I was thinking when I look back. It seems so long ago now. We tried living together but it didn't work out."

It was Maxine's honesty, her refusal to duck and dodge the truth that impressed Rae most. She was really starting to like her. If things were different, Maxine would be one of the women who could become one of her closest girlfriends. Quinn was lucky to know someone like her.

"Do you still love Quinn?" Rae asked the question, watching the woman's face.

"You don't fool around with the questions, do you?"

"I guess not. Do you still love him, Maxine? I need to know." Rae's heart was pounding like a drum and her hands were sweating. This was the Big Question.

Maxine patted her on the hand, grinning. "Relax, Rae. Yes, I love him and I believe I always will. But it's not the kind of love you build a life on. I have a good man, Taylor, who loves me very much, and a beautiful son. What more could I want? I can't remember when I've been happier, more complete."

Rae visibly sagged in her seat, the muscles in her face relaxed into a relieved smile. "Honestly, you had me worried. I thought you wanted him back. In fact, I didn't know what to think, especially since you had this past life with him. And a child."

"Yeah, we have some history and a child but I know he's not the man for me," Maxine said. "I love Quinn but I'm not *in* love with him. There's a difference. We had our moment and it didn't work. He hurt me when he left me to come back East to be with Niki in New York. But I forgave him. Or maybe I didn't."

"What do you mean?" Rae's eyebrows hiked up.

"I hurt him, too. My timing about telling him he had a son was wrong. I hurt him by keeping that knowledge away from him for so long. Three years. I waited so long and I don't really know why. I told him after Niki's funeral, when he was at the lowest point of his life. It was wrong and cruel. Maybe I wanted to hurt him like he had me . . ."

Rae saw Maxine fight back tears, swallowing hard to shut down the waterworks before they could really get started. She covered her face for a moment with her hands and then pulled them away, apologizing.

"You care a lot for him, don't you?" Rae asked, feeling the woman's pain.

"Yes, I do. Don't you?"

Rae nodded a couple of times as if reassuring herself that it was true. "I love him, Maxine. He's something special."

Maxine looked at her, eyes glistening. "Quinn is all that. Believe me. It's hard to meet men, at least good men. I'm not saying he's Mr. Right, I don't know that because I'm not you, but I can definitely say he's not Mr. Wrong. Quinn has some rough edges. We all do. But he has a lot to offer some lucky woman. Be patient. Work with him and you'll have a real keeper. Let all his pain ebb out. Let his love for you grow. He's complex, temperamental, and sometimes hard to understand. Girl, even with all that, Quinn is all man and worth his weight in gold."

They sat there, finishing off their food and coffee. Neither saying anything. Thinking about all that had been said before.

Suddenly, Maxine tapped her finger on the table and asked if she thought Quinn would ever write or play again. The one thing, other than love, that kept him balanced.

"I'm working on him," Rae said, feeling certain. "I'll have him back doing his music thing before long. I know how much it means to him. It's a part of the reason he's so nutty right now. Not playing.''

Maxine shook her fork at Rae, chuckling. ''I'm glad we talked. You're just what he needs. Even if he doesn't know it yet.''

They laughed at that, paid for the food, and left. On the street, amid the crowds, Rae turned and hugged Maxine, her lips brushing against the woman's cheek. Then she whispered two words, lovingly and sincerely. ''Thank you.''

Chapter Nineteen

"Well, little man, looks like it's just us fellas," Quinn said to Jamel as he took Jamel's lunch plate away. Maxine and Rae had left together about an hour earlier after Max dropped off Jamel. They were almost too chummy for his taste. Made a brother nervous. "What do you wanna do today, J?" He put the dishes in the sink.

"Play in the snow!"

Quinn chuckled. "That out there isn't really snow anymore, it's a mess. But how 'bout if we do some shopping of our own?"

"Can I get a game for my Nintendo?" His eyes widened.

"Early Christmas gift?" Quinn teased, with a raised brow.

Jamel nodded shyly.

"Awright. But don't tell your mother. It'll be our

secret.'' He stuck his hand out and Jamel gave him a five. ''Come on. Get your coat. There's a great game store on Fourteenth Street. We'll walk.''

''In the snow?'' Jamel asked, bright lights twinkling in his eyes.

''Yeah,'' Quinn conceded. ''If that's what you want to call it,'' he said under his breath.

Jamel went darting off to get his coat.

''Don't forget your boots!'' Quinn shouted behind him. He shook his head and chuckled. ''Snow.''

''Daddy?''

''Yeah, buddy.'' Quinn stopped at the corner for the red light.

''Is Miss Rae your . . . girlfriend?''

Whoa. ''Uh, yeah. She is. Is that cool with you?'' He looked down at his son.

Jamel's small face screwed up for a moment of consideration. ''I guess.'' He gazed up at his father. ''Is she nicer to you than Mommy?''

''Why do you think she's nicer than Mommy?'' he asked gently.

'' 'Cause . . . she's here with you and Mommy's not . . . and maybe it's 'cause you don't like Mommy . . . and me.''

Quinn's heart felt as if it had seized in his chest. Once on the other side of the street, Quinn led Jamel over to the front of Virgin Records under the shelter of the overhang. He bent down to Jamel's eye level.

''Listen to me, J.'' He braced Jamel's shoulders. ''Me and your mom . . .'' What could he say that would make sense, when sometimes he wasn't too sure of what went wrong himself? "Sometimes, things don't work out between two people." He swallowed. How would Remy have counseled him? What had he said to him so many times when he'd come to Remy and asked what had he done so wrong to make his mother leave?

"Remember when you were here during the summer and you were telling me about your friend Carlos in your kindergarten class?"

Jamel nodded.

"And remember how you said you two had an argument and you were real upset because he was your best friend?"

"Yes."

"And I told you that happens with friends. Sometimes they don't agree, sometimes without thinking they hurt each other's feelings. Right? But if you were really friends, you would make up and say sorry and sometimes the friendship changes because of what was said or done . . . and you could be friends, but a different kind of friend. Like you and Carlos are now."

"I said sorry, like you told me to do. And I still talk to him when I see him in the lunchroom. But we're not best friends anymore. He's in 103 and I'm in 101. Andre is my best friend now."

"Do you feel bad that you and Carlos aren't best friends anymore?"

Jamel shrugged. "Sometimes. But he has new friends, too. Sometimes we play in the yard together."

"That's kinda like what happened with me and your mom, J. We had a disagreement about some things and even after we said sorry, things changed. And it has nothing to do with you, son. We both love you very much. Very much. Understand."

Jamel looked into his father's eyes and slowly bobbed his head. Quinn smiled and hugged him tight, hoping he'd said all the right words. This father thing wasn't easy.

Jamel wiggled away. "Is this the game store?" Jamel asked, his mind already on more important issues.

Quinn stood and chuckled. "Naw, right around the corner. And you know what? Since you've been so good, you can get two."

"Yippee!"

After about an hour in the game store, then on to the pizza parlor for a quick bite, and Virgin Records to pick up some CDs for Quinn—even if he didn't play he never stopped loving the music—they started back home.

It was about two blocks before Quinn's house, when she spotted them. Her thin hand fluttered to her chest when she saw the handsome pair together—father and son.

Without thinking she kept them in her sight from the opposite side of the street until they reached a house and went inside. She stared at the house, the closed door, and debated about what to do, what she should have done long ago.

She wasn't sure how long she'd stood there in the cold, pacing the few steps back and forth trying to summon up the courage to cross the street. When she glanced at the house, they were coming out with an old woman from the ground floor door. She watched the woman hug the little boy and wave as they entered a black Jeep and drove away.

Tentatively, she crossed the street, not sure what she would do when she got there. She opened the short, black iron gate and walked to the front door. For a moment she felt like fleeing, just letting well enough alone.

"Who's there?" Mrs. Finch called out from the window, stopping her in her tracks.

Startled, she turned to the window and saw the face of the old woman peering back at her. It was now or never.

"I . . . my name is Vera . . . I . . . Could I speak with you . . . for a minute?"

Maxine and Rae had yet to return from their shopping spree when Quinn dropped Jamel off at his grandmother's house, promising to come for him the following day. After chatting briefly with Mrs. Sherman he headed back home, wondering how the two women had made out.

Rae had been damned near secretive when he'd talked to her about it the night before, as if they were concocting something. He wondered what secrets of his past Max would reveal, if anything, and what Rae would have to say about their current situation.

It was a strange predicament to be in, but he wasn't trying to front, trying to hide anything from anyone. Yeah, he still felt a little something, something in his heart for Max, he always would. She'd been there for him for as long as he could remember. And he had to admit that he felt those old waves of warmth whenever he saw her. It still hurt every time he thought about how she'd deceived him by not telling him about Jamel, but he was getting beyond that, too. She'd been holding up her end in seeing that he had a relationship with his son, even with her husband, Taylor, in the picture. That couldn't be easy for either of them. He knew he had a hard pill to swallow knowing that some other man was raising his son. Yeah, he definitely had to keep his hand in.

Hey, it was like what Remy drummed into his head out on the boat. Be patient and let things work themselves out.

He pulled into the last available spot on the block, thankful that he wouldn't have to jump up in the morning to move his Jeep. He put his key in the door and was just about to walk into his apartment when Mrs. Finch called out to him from downstairs.

He groaned. She couldn't possibly want him to run any errands. The front of the house was clear of snow and ice, her refrigerator was stocked. He'd taken her quilts to the laundry, and he'd cleaned out the basement weeks ago. He closed his eyes.

"Yeees, Mrs. Finch."

Slowly, she walked up the stairs, something she rarely did, and met him at the top of the landing. She had an anxious look on her face that put Quinn immediately on alert.

"What's wrong? Are you feelin' okay?" He went to her and took her hand and she made the last step.

She looked up at him, knew what she had to say to him would once again turn his world upside down. She'd prayed on it during the last hour, asked for guidance and the right words to say. She'd simply have to let go and let God.

"Son," she began, "I think we need to go inside so we can sit and talk."

Quinn's heart began to pound. He could tell whatever she had to say was nothing but trouble. He didn't want trouble. Not again.

Chapter Twenty

Quinn sat on the edge of the couch. He could feel his entire body trembling with rage, disbelief, and so many other emotions he couldn't give a name to. He ran his hands through his locks, then across his face. His chest was in a knot, he could barely breathe.

He stalked over to his liquor cabinet and poured a glass of Jack Daniels, downing it in one long gulp, then refilling it before the first splash had hit his stomach.

His body shuddered as deep, wrenching sobs gripped him and shook him like a lone leaf on a tree. Tears spilled down his cheeks in a steady stream. Suddenly he spun around and threw the glass across the room, smashing it against the wall.

"Liar!" he roared like a wounded beast. "Damn you to hell!" He snatched up his jacket and stormed out, pulling away from Mrs. Finch when she tried to stop him from getting into his car.

She watched in horror as Quinn tore recklessly away from the curb and sped away, disappearing from sight within minutes.

"Oh, Lawd, oh, Lawd, what have I done? Watch over my boy, please," she cried and stumbled back into the house.

His eyes were bloodshot as he stalked into Encore like a madman, demanding to know from the skeleton staff were this Vera was.

Stunned customers whispered among themselves, couples pulled closer together, trying to steer clear of Quinn, who moved like a storm out of control, wheeling between tables, heading for the kitchen.

He pushed open the swinging doors with such force that the line of cooks and dishwashers scattered like startled birds.

His reddened eyes tore across the tight space looking for her. "Where is she?" he demanded. He pushed past one of the waiters, to the back of the room.

"What the hell is going on in here?" came the hard mean voice of the security guard from behind Quinn, followed by a steely hand on his arm.

Quinn tossed the offending hand away as if it were an annoying fly. The guard stumbled into one of the cooks.

"It's okay, Mike," came the now familiar reed-thin voice from the back of the kitchen.

Quinn zeroed in on her, a million thoughts tumbling through his mind at once. He was breathing hard, trying to control this level of rage he'd never before felt. The overwhelming sensation of it, the control it had taken over his mind, frightened him with its power. It was then he knew from where true violence emerged.

Slowly Vera walked toward him, her eyes unwavering. The staff moved to the far side of the cramped space like the parting of the Red Sea.

She stood in front of him, stood accused of all the things she saw reflected in his eyes. She raised her chin a notch.

He pointed his finger at her, his face twisted in an angry mask. "You take back what you said," he hissed. "Eat every lying word of it."

"It's not a lie, Quinten," she said softly.

He blinked away a new wave of tears. His nostrils flared as he tried to suck in air.

"There's so much I need to finally tell you," she continued, then paused for a moment. "Will you at least listen to what I have to say? Please." When he didn't respond, didn't move, she continued. "We can talk in the back room." She moved past him, past the shocked faces, unsure, but determined to face whatever transpired between them.

Quinn followed her out, wondering what other lies she would tell behind closed doors. He'd hear the old bird out, make sure she was clear about staying away from him and anyone he knew, and then he would leave. Simple.

He watched her walk in front of him and a distant memory flashed through his head: the walk, the tilt of her head, the many nights he'd watch her, no, his mother, walk out the door.

Vera opened a narrow door at the far end of the

dimly lit corridor. She stepped inside. Quinn stepped in and closed the door.

"Whaddya mean coming around my place . . . talkin' about you're my mother. You been eying me since the first time I walked into this joint. I don't know what your scheme is, but back off."

Vera reached into the recesses of her bra and pulled out a pack of Salem cigarettes.

Quinn's head spun. *"Pass me my smokes, will you, Quinten?"* his mother had asked, as she stepped into her shoes, ready to leave again, this time for the rest of the night. Quinn had taken the pack of Salem from the battered dresser and handed them to her. *"You goin' out again?"*

"Told you about gettin' into adult business. You just look after your sister." She had taken the cigarettes, tapped one out, and stuck it in the corner of her bloodred lips, turned, and walked out the door.

His head began to pound as he watched her light the cigarette now, holding it in the corner of her mouth . . . as she'd always done. *No. You're dead. Dead.*

"You was only sixteen . . . you and Lacy, when I left," she began. She blew a cloud of smoke into the air. "Know it wasn't right what I done, but I didn't have no choice, son."

He flinched. "Don't you call me son," he said from between his teeth. "Don't you dare."

For a moment she looked away from the pure hatred in his eyes. "I wasn't no good to you or your sister . . . the way I was back then, no more than a kid myself." She turned away. "Then . . . it was the drugs, the drugs, men, and more drugs. Some days I didn't know if I was coming or going, just knew I needed my hit to get through the day." She turned to face him and pulled in a breath. "And . . . I had to get them . . . any way I could."

He shut his eyes as the painful memories nearly consumed him. The nights he would lie awake, hear Lacy crying in her sleep, both of them wondering when or if their mother was coming back.

"I know you ain't gonna understand this . . . or believe it, but I did it because I loved you both. Loved you too much to let you see what I'd become. You two was the only things I did decent in my life, was decent in my life, and with what little of myself I had left I knew I couldn't poison you." She took a step toward him. "It was the only thing I could do. . . ."

"Shut up! Just shut up." He backed away from her. He didn't want to believe the lies, the unthinkable, but deep in his heart he knew she spoke the ugly truth. "You think walking out on us, just leaving us like some forgotten garbage was the only thing you could do? Do you know what you did to us? Do you have any idea? Do you know how scared we were? Do you know the . . . the . . . things I had to do to survive, take care of Lacy?"

He turned away and began to pace the tight quarters. "All my life I figured it was something I'd done, hadn't done, that if I was a better son you would have stayed. That you would have loved us."

"Quinten—"

"Don't you say anything," he growled, whirling toward her. "Not now. You abandoned us." His voice cracked. "Know what that's like, to feel unworthy, too afraid to trust anyone, care about anyone because you know they're gonna leave you? Know what it's like to have your childhood stolen, 'cause you had to become a man too soon? But we survived . . . without you.''

Vera hung her head. She deserved everything he said and more. ''There ain't been a day gone by that I haven't thought about you and your sister, prayed that you two was okay.''

He laughed nastily. ''Yeah. Your prayers were just about as useless as you. Lacy's dead. And so are you.''

She visibly paled and sank down into a rickety, wooden chair. She covered her face with her hands, as deep soul-robbing sobs wracked her body. Suddenly she looked small and weak, not the monster he'd conjured in his mind.

Quinn watched her, wanting to grab her, hurt her some more, crush her heart the way she'd done to them. And at the same time he wanted her to hold him, tell him it wasn't his fault, that he'd been a good son and brother.

''I . . . I'm so sorry. Sorry for everything I done to you, to your sister. Oh, God,'' she uttered between her tears. ''I know you can't forgive me. I just want you to try to understand. It wasn't your fault. Never.'' She looked up at him with pleading eyes. Eyes that reflected his own pain and despair. ''I was wrong what I done and I've paid for it every day of my life. 'Cause I just walked out without ever telling y'all that I loved you.''

Something inside of him twisted and rose to his throat. The vision before him became blurred. He turned, and on unsteady legs headed for the door.

''Quinten, pleeease . . .'' came her strangled cry.

He turned and she reached for him, her arms extended just as he'd envisioned for far too long. Her thin fingers grabbed his arms and held him as if he was now the only thing that could hold her up.

Quinn looked at her, saw all that she'd done, all he and Lacy had been through. Slowly, he peeled her fingers away as she collapsed to the floor, and he turned and walked out to the keening sound of his name.

Quinn drove around for hours, his mind spinning, his emotions out of reach. His *mother.* How many nights had he wished that she'd walk through the door, tell them she'd been on a long trip, but she was back and everything would be all right again? How many streets had he walked, hoping and dreading that he would see her walk out of one of those tenements? Hoping that he could let go of his fears, learn to trust, allow others to get close to him? He lived his life in fear. A fear he shielded behind street savvy and bravado. Always afraid that at any moment someone would find him out, pull his card, and show him for what he really was—someone who doubted his worth—as a boy, a son, a man.

When Maxine saw Quinn standing outside her mother's apartment door, she had a momentary flash of déjà vu—the night he appeared on her doorstep in San Francisco with the police settlement letter about Lacy. He had the same wounded look in his eyes then.

She stepped aside and let him in, leading him to the living room. Without a word she sat down and waited for him to speak, unable to imagine what could have happened. And when he finally told her, that his mother was not dead, but very much alive, you could have knocked her over with a puff of air.

She leaned forward. "What? Alive . . . after all this . . ." She squeezed her eyes shut, recalling all too well what the three of them—Quinn, Lacy, and she—had gone through during those years. Quinn dropping out of school to work with Remy, so that Lacy could stay in. Pretending that their mom was still around so the social workers wouldn't come and take them away. The nights that Max would bring leftovers because they didn't have enough to eat. And all along, she was alive.

Maxine looked up at him and her heart nearly broke in two when she saw the thin line of tears course down his cheeks. She reached across the space and touched his hand. "What did she say, Q? Did she explain why?"

He turned away, ashamed of showing this weak side of himself. But if not to Max, then who? "Yeah, she explained." He told her what Vera gave as her explanation. "All a bunch of bull, Max." He pulled away from her grasp and stood.

She came up behind him, pressed her head to his back, and put her arms around his waist. The familiarity of it all was bittersweet. And she realized at that moment, that as much as she would always love a part of Quinten Parker, this was no longer her role, and had not been for a long time.

"Q," she said softly, stepping away.

Slowly he turned around and pulled in a long breath. "For as long as we've known each other, I always made it easy for you to turn to me, come to me with your worries, your joys, your ideas, your pains. And I realize now that I did all that because it was the only way I could have a piece of you in my life. Make it easy for you, accessible." She lowered her head for a moment, not wanting to hurt him any more than he had been, but needing him to know and needing to say the words. "But we've all grown up now, Q. You're not that same man and I'm not that same woman. And as much as it may seem like I'm the one to turn to, I'm not. It's just familiar."

He swallowed hard. "So . . . what are you saying?"

"I'm saying that maybe it's finally time to let go of the past, as hard as it may be. You have a woman who loves you. A good woman. The right woman for you. If you give her half a chance, she'll listen. She'll help you make it all right again. She needs you and you need her now."

And as he stood there feeling the familiar ties begin to unravel, the ground shift from beneath his feet, he knew deep in his heart that she was right.

He reached out and touched her cheek, nodding slowly in acceptance. "Thank you," he said softly, "for letting go."

"Always luv ya, Q," she said tenderly.

He smiled and placed a tender kiss on her forehead. "You, too."

As she watched him walk away she had a real strong feeling that Quinten Parker was finally on his way to being all right.

Chapter Twenty-one

Rae was in the midst of putting her few purchases under the tree, thinking about the afternoon she'd spent with Maxine, and the revelations that were presented to her, the new things she'd learned about Quinn.

Maxine had turned out to be nothing like whom she'd imagined. She wasn't just another "baby's mama" but a true woman in every sense of the word. On the way home, she'd even told her about her brand-new pregnancy and how excited she was about having Taylor's child. She had solidly laid her fears to rest. It was up to Rae now as to how she and Quinn proceeded, not the ghosts of Nikita and Maxine who would determine their future. She only hoped that Quinn would feel the same way.

She was just about to call him, when her doorbell rang. Inwardly she smiled, knowing that it must be him, wanting to get the inside scoop on what had transpired. But she quickly discovered that wasn't his reason for the visit.

The instant she saw him, she knew something was terribly wrong, that something had happened to Jamel or Mrs. Finch.

"Quinn, what is it?" She searched his stoic face, stepping aside to let him in. She touched his arm, but he kept walking as if she weren't there.

Mechanically, he walked into the living room and sat on one of the large pillows on the floor, his arms between his knees, head bowed.

She hurried over to him, kneeling down. "Baby, what is it? You're scaring me. Whatever it is, just tell me," she urged, her mind now running at full speed.

Slowly he looked up into her eyes, which were filled with worry, concern . . . and, yes, love. He swallowed hard and began to force out the words, one by one, needing to say them, release the unbearable weight that rested on his chest.

When he was done he realized that he was gripping Rae's hand and that the simple gesture had somehow helped him to work through it all, relive it again without feeling so terribly alone. He looked into her eyes and saw the tears shimmering there. She raised his hand to her lips and tenderly kissed it.

"Are you okay?"

"I don't know. I don't know how I feel, what I think. After it happened I went to see Maxine and—"

"Maxine?" She shook her head in confusion. "W—why did you go to Maxine, Quinn?"

"Doing what I've always done, Rae, going to something familiar," he admitted.

"Why didn't you think you could come to me with . . . with something like this?" she asked, the hurt evident in her voice. "I mean, I know you and Maxine have a history, but—"

"Baby, I wasn't thinking, not really." He cupped her cheek. "She told me as much."

"Told you what, Quinn?" she asked hesitantly.

"Told me that I had to stop looking for something familiar, something easy, something I wouldn't have to give too much of myself to in return for all the things I needed." He paused a beat. "She told me we're different people now with new and different lives, and it was time to move on." He looked deep into her eyes. "And she was right, Rae."

"Are you ready to move on, Quinn? Really?" She squeezed his hands between hers. "Will you run back to Maxine whenever there's a crisis in your life, some accomplishment, or joy to share? Are you truly past it all . . . past Maxine?"

He didn't hesitate a beat. "Yes, Rae. I am. You've got to believe that."

She sat back on her haunches, relieved now that maybe she could help with what the real reason for his visit was.

"What are you going to do about . . . your mother?" she asked gently.

He shook his head, his features suddenly contorting. "I don't have a mother."

"Quinn, I know you may not want to hear this, but your . . . she reached out to you for a reason. Guilt is a heavy burden, Quinn. You and I both know that. Sometimes we believe we do things for all the right reasons. Sometimes they're selfish reasons. Sometimes we're so involved in our own world, our own issues, we can no longer see how what we do affects others." Her voice wavered as she thought of herself, what she'd done in her life, to her husband and daughter, thinking of how many sleepless nights she'd wished that she could turn back the clock, regain all the time she'd lost with them. But she couldn't. No one could.

"I'd give anything to get it all back, Quinn. Let them know how sorry I was. How I regretted the times I left them. Most of us don't get a second chance to make things right, to make amends. You have that chance, Quinn."

"It's . . . too late. Too many years. Too much pain, lost time, lives . . ."

"It's never too late," she said in an urgent whisper. "Never too late to change, to forgive and be forgiven. When I met you, Quinten Parker, I'd finally found something besides my music that could fill my life, that was worthwhile, that gave my days new meaning. It didn't hurt so much anymore. You did that for me. And I've slowly begun to realize that there was nothing we could have done, Quinn," she said softly. "You couldn't have stopped your mother from leaving, couldn't have stopped what happened to your sister or your wife. Just as I couldn't have stopped what happened to Sterling and Akia.

"And we can either choose to accept the blame, the guilt for something we had no control over, because it's easier to be the martyr, to keep people at bay, our emotions tucked away and out of reach so we can't be hurt—or we can choose the hard road where we expose ourselves to all the possibilities, the joys, and the pains of life."

"I don't know how, Rae. How can I just forget it all as if it never happened?"

"You don't forget. You'll never forget, the good or the bad. But you forgive, so you can release the burden you've been carrying. Forgive your sister for unintentionally being in the wrong place at the wrong time and leaving you. Forgive Nikita for driving at night, for not seeing the oncoming car, for leaving you. Forgive your mother for letting her weakness take her away from you. If you can do that, finally do that, the healing you've been searching for will finally begin."

The words seeped into his pores, spread through him like a healing elixir. Slowly his heart began to open, his soul began to stir. That was the key all along. Deep in his heart he blamed them. Each of them. And he carried the blame, the anger, and turned it on himself. Taking the easy way out by accepting responsibility for something he could not control, rather than find fault with those to whom he'd given his love. Finally, all the pieces were falling into place. The elusive part of himself that he'd lost was now within reach.

Tenderly he gathered Rae in his arms, pressing her body close to his, allowing the full essence of this woman to become a part of him, enter him, letting her love soothe the wounds, make him whole. And it was then he knew just how right Maxine had been. Rae was willing to accept him with all his baggage, his dents and scuffs, and drag him into tomorrow kicking and screaming. She was willing to work as hard as he, not wanting him to change but to grow, right along with her.

"I . . . I love you," he whispered. "I love you, Rae," he repeated, the words like a prayer that had been answered.

Her heart filled, and an incredible warmth, a singular joy coursed through her body. She leaned back, looking into his dark eyes. "And I'll never leave you," she promised.

He touched her lips with his, sealing their pact, their bond, their future, and hoped that her promise would remain true.

Chapter Twenty-two

Rae thought she'd be a nervous wreck preparing Christmas brunch for Maxine and her husband. But the minute Maxine came through the door she insisted on pitching in, and Taylor was a doll, doting on his wife as if she were royalty. She could see why Maxine was mad about him. What was really special was that it was Rae's first Christmas with Quinn, the first she or Quinn had celebrated in three years. And it was the first time he'd celebrated Christmas with his son, who'd been up since dawn squealing over his toys under Quinn's tree. It truly was a day to be thankful.

Quinn eased up behind her and planted a kiss on the back of her neck. "You've gotten real comfortable in my kitchen," he teased, wrapping his arms around her waist and erotically rotating his pelvis against her bottom.

Rae playfully slapped his hands. "Quinn," she said in a hushed voice. "We have company. Suppose somebody sees us."

He reached over her shoulder and snatched a carrot stick from a tray. "Then I'd have to confess that I'm crazy about you and can't keep my hands off you."

She turned into his arms, looked coyly up at him. "That's why I love you, Quinten Parker. You always know what to say to a girl." She pecked him lightly on the lips. "Now scram. You're in my way."

"The lady of the house has spoken." He patted her bottom and returned to his guests.

The afternoon went off without a hitch as each of them shared war stories and anecdotes, with both Quinn and Taylor trying valiantly to help Jamel put his erector set together. Even Gail stopped by to drop off gifts—and to get an up-close look at Maxine, Rae secretly knew. And with much prodding from Quinn, Mrs. Finch joined them and contributed dessert.

Maxine and Taylor had promised to join Maxine's mother for dinner and to bring her grandson so she could spoil him some more, Maxine said as they put on their coats and began to leave.

While Quinn helped Jamel to the car with all of his Christmas loot, Maxine turned to Rae.

"I'm really glad I met you," she said sincerely. "You're good for him. I see the changes."

Rae smiled. "He's good for me, too."

Maxine reached over and hugged her. "Be happy," she whispered in her ear. "Be there for him and he'll never let you down."

"I will. I promise."

* * *

Quinn listened to Rae's easy breathing as they lay spooned against each other, after making slow, passionate love. While she slept, he stroked her hair, studied her face. The events of the day played back in slow motion, each scene, each smiling face, the true happiness he felt. Rae brought that to his life. For that he would be forever grateful.

The past few months had been hard, almost unbearable at times, but he'd gotten through them. Through the fire, as Rae had said, to the safety on the other side, and she'd been there waiting. And she deserved the best of him, all of him, and in order to do that, to come to her fully, he had to complete the last piece of the puzzle.

Quinn sat in his Jeep for a good half hour, staring at the entrance to Encore. He knew she was inside, he'd seen her go in. He started to go after her then, but he had no idea what he would say to her. He still didn't know as he pushed through the doors.

"We're not open yet, sir," one of the waitresses immediately informed him, recognizing him from the episode a few days earlier. She didn't want any trouble.

"I'm looking for Vera Parker."

"Look, Mister, I said we're not open. I think you need to leave."

He ignored her and continued into the restaurant. It would be easy to take her warning and just leave. He didn't do easy these days. He looked around, hoping that he would spot her before the frightened girl called for backup.

There she was, bent over a table, washing it down and replacing the used ashtrays with clean ones. His stomach knotted. Tentatively he headed in her direction and took a seat at the table next to the one she was working on. Surprise, then a sense of what appeared to be relief, which was quickly replaced by uncertainty, danced across her worn face.

For the first time he could see beyond his anger and hurt to the devastation that had painted itself permanently into her features. The eyes that had no sparkle, the stoop to the once proud shoulders. Her body spoke of the abuse she'd put it through, and all around her hung a veil of aloneness. How he understood that feeling. This is what her choices had done to her.

"I didn't think I'd see you again."

"We need to talk," Quinn responded in a flat monotone, still hoping that the words would come to him.

Vera looked around, then slowly pulled out a chair opposite him and sat. She clasped her hands tightly in front of her. "I can't tell you how sorry I am. I—"

"I don't need to hear sorry . . . Vera. I need to hear why. Why did you do it? Why did you let 'the life' become more important than me and Lacy? And I don't wanna hear nothin' but the truth. I need to know *why* I am, who I am. Who you really are. Why we never knew our father. Answers to all the questions you were never around long enough to give."

She locked and unlocked her fingers, trying to figure out where to begin, how it all started. It was so long ago, sometimes it seemed like a distant memory, at others as clear as yesterday. *Start at the beginning. Tell him,* an inner voice whispered.

"I was young," she began, her voice a bit unsteady. "Only sixteen when I met your father. He was going on twenty." She smiled tremulously. "I thought he was the most handsome man I'd ever seen. And the fact that he had an eye for Vera Johnson was more than I could have ever dreamed of. I think I fell in love with your daddy the first time I laid eyes on him behind the counter at the movie theater," she said wistfully.

"We started seeing each other regular. He used to treat me so good. Always had a kind word and a gentle touch." She paused for a moment and looked away. "When I turned up pregnant, he didn't run off like some of them other boys had done to friends of mine. Not Jake Parker. He told me no child of his would grow up without a daddy." She swallowed hard, the memories of that first and only love washing over her in waves. "With my folks being dead and all, my old aunt didn't want to have nothing to do with taking care of a teenage girl and her baby. Jake said we didn't need nobody but each other. So we ran off and got married. I'd just turned eighteen."

Quinn tried to imagine his mother as a young girl in love, away from home with a child on the way. How she could have turned from that girl into the woman she'd become. But he would listen, as Remy had wisely advised. Listen and let things unfold.

"We struggled. Barely made it some days, living from place to place, having to move every time the rent was due. Jake found odd jobs, here and there, but nothing really solid. It was hard on black men back then, still is. And when two babies came instead of one, it took a toll on both of us.'' She stopped as if that was the end of her story, as if that would explain it all.

''You still haven't told me why you did it,'' Quinn ground out.

Vera snapped from her musings and focused on Quinn. *He looks so much like Jake,* she thought suddenly.

''It's hard on a man when he can't provide for his family. Takes the man out of him,'' she said in a voice filled with regret. ''I watched that proud man day by day become reduced. Come home beaten by the world. And when he looked at the three of us, all he saw was a battle he couldn't win.''

Quinn's pulse beat with anxiety waiting to hear the words.

''One day Jake said he was going to look for work. He left that morning . . . and I never seen him again.'' Her eyes momentarily filled, and she blinked the tears away.

Quinn shook his head in disgust. ''So he was no better than you.''

She reached for him, saw him recoil, and slowly pulled her hand back. ''It wasn't like that. Your father was a good man, a decent man,'' she insisted.

''Yeah, a man who walked away from his family.''

''I started getting letters, a few months after he disappeared,'' she continued, refusing to allow her memories of Jake to be turned into something ugly. He didn't deserve that. ''Plain, white envelopes with no return address, with a few dollars tucked inside.''

''What did the letters say?'' Quinn asked.

''That he was doing the best thing he could. And that for as long as he was breathing he would send us something. But he could no longer face us, be a man in our eyes. You and your sister was growing like weeds and the few dollars that your daddy sent wasn't enough. So I started working at a club, as a waitress, and after a while even that wasn't enough. Y'all were getting big, needing things. Then one day, the letters stopped coming. I waited and waited, prayed and waited." Her voice broke into jagged edges. "And finally I realized I wasn't never gonna hear from him again. That it was up to me now. A man at the club told me a way I could make some more money if I really wanted to. I started . . . giving myself to men . . . for money. Started taking the drugs so I wouldn't feel anything. Went on for years, till the habit got so bad I needed all the money for the drugs.

"One night I came home and you were sitting on that raggedy couch. When I walked through the door, full of drugs, booze . . . and saw the hurt, disappointed look in your eyes, I knew I couldn't stay, couldn't never see you look at me like that again."

The image of her in that red dress, her lipstick smeared and her stockings twisted around her legs, loomed before him. He remembered how he helped her to bed, put the cover over her, and shut the door so Lacy wouldn't see her. How powerless he felt.

"I could have helped you," he said, his voice vibrating in his chest. "I would have if you'd let me."

"You couldn't have helped me. Nobody could. Not then. I saw how strong you were, and I knew that if I left you'd make a way. I knew that."

"All this time, all these years I spent not knowing. Not understanding. Lacy and I did the best we could. Tried to make a life."

"Tell me about her . . . about you."

He gave her brief snatches, blurry glimpses of the

life they lived, the teens, then adults they'd become, keeping most of the precious memories to himself, denying her that one wish. And as she listened she realized what her choice had ultimately done. It robbed them all. Robbed them of a time in their lives they could never regain. And just as her words to Quinn could not make up for what she'd put them through, what she heard now would never fill the voids that her absence had created. There was no going back. All they could hope to do now was find a way to move forward—finally.

Slowly Quinn looked up at her, surprised to see tears and a look of resolve on her face as she wearily stood.

"I know you won't believe this, but you're blessed in a way. Blessed with strength and courage and most of all memories of a time I will never know, can never be a part of, that will be denied to me forever. And for all that I've done that is my greatest regret, the time I lost being a mother to my children. You're a good man . . . son. A man any mother . . . would be proud to call her own. Even me." She turned to walk away, doing all she could have done and hoping that he would finally be all right and maybe one day find it in his heart to forgive her.

"Mama . . ." The foreign word struggled up from his throat.

She turned around, her heart hammering in her chest. She tugged on her bottom lip with her teeth, not knowing what to expect.

"I . . . I know I'll never forget what you did." He swallowed, looked away for a moment, thought about all the hard roads he'd traveled, the fires he'd survived, and he knew he could get through this, too—by finally letting go. "But I can start trying to forgive."

Tentatively she reached for him, then stopped halfway. And then she felt something she hadn't in longer than she could remember—the touch of her son's hand slipping into hers.

Chapter Twenty-three

Winter had finally released its hold on the city and spring had burst forth with what seemed a new sense of vitality, Quinn thought as he tiptoed from his bedroom, leaving Rae still curled in sleep.

He smiled on his way down the stairs. Everything seemed new and better, different somehow, and so was he. He knew having Rae in his life was a big part of it. She'd stuck by him, through his tirades, his sullenness, his uncertainty, and ultimately his evolution. *Patience.* Rae had it in spades.

No doubt their relationship wasn't perfect, but what was? All you could do was give it your best and be the best person you could. That's what he was striving for.

He entered the living room and looked at the piano. The keys not having been touched by him in far too long. He still heard melodies in his head, saw his fingers working the ivories. Lately the same chords, the same sound kept reverberating in his head, like in the old days when he would toil for hours until he got it right. He'd told Rae months ago that he was working out a new tune in his head, but he never did more than that. But more and more the music kept calling him, stirring him up inside.

Warily he walked toward the piano, stroked the smooth wood. For an instant, his chest tightened as flashes of the past tried to claim him. And finally he did with this last hurdle what he'd done with all the others—stepped over it.

Slowly he sat down and raised the covering of the keys. His insides warmed as he gingerly placed his fingers in position, trying to locate that space inside him that would make the keys sing. The first string of notes were off key, but he didn't stop as the melody that had been playing in his head began to come to life through his fingers. He closed his eyes and let the music flow from him, saw the notes dance in his mind, the images that he was forever setting free. The haunting melody traveled the length of the scale, varying tempo and speed as his mind and body became one with the music.

Rae stood silently in the doorway, her hand covering her mouth, her eyes wet with tears. The music was as painful as it was beautiful, but what was even more inspiring was that he was truly alive again. The demons were finally banished and the music that he played came from the soul of a healed man.

"That's the piece that's been missing," Rae said softly as the song drew to a gentle close.

Quinn turned over his shoulder as she approached. She sat beside him on the bench. "It was beautiful," she said with genuine sincerity. "I know how hard it's been for you."

"I'm finally past that now, Rae," he said with resolve. "It took me a while, but I'm past it. You know my mother talked about how the time lost that could never be regained is the greatest of regrets. I don't want to have any more regrets, Rae. I want to use the time I have, that we have, to the fullest."

"You don't know how long I've waited to hear you say that."

He grinned mischievously. "I think I have an idea."

She lowered her head for a moment, contemplating if it was too soon, but decided to try anyway. "While I was listening to you play, I could see the lyrics forming in front of my eyes. The perfect words to go with a perfect piece of music."

Quinn angled his head to the side. "What are you saying . . . exactly?"

Rae pursed her lips. "I was hoping . . . that maybe you would consider . . . us putting the words and the music together."

"Me and you, like a team? Like Ashford and Simpson?"

She grinned. "Yeah, something like that. What do you think?"

He pulled in a deep breath, wondering what it would be like to work with this feisty woman who could be as stubborn and headstrong as he. He knew they'd battle before it was all said and done. But, he was up for a good fight.

"I think I like the sound of that."

Rae squealed in delight and wrapped her arms around his neck, nearly knocking them both off the bench.

"Lindsay and Parker," she announced, looking him in the eye.

"Parker and Lindsay," he countered.

"Hmm. We'll have to take a vote on that," she returned, being intentionally difficult.

Quinn put his arms around her waist and pulled her close. He looked into her eyes and saw all the possibilities reflected there. He saw tomorrow and the day after. Him and Rae.

"How 'bout Parker and Parker?" he asked quietly.

Rae's animated expression suddenly became still. Her eyes widened. Her voice shook over the racing beat of her heart. "Quinn . . . are you asking me to . . . marry you?"

"Yeah, I am, Rae. Will you? Will you share the rest of my life with me and whatever our life together will bring? Can you?" As he waited for her response he realized he'd never been so afraid in his life, afraid of what he would do if she said no.

Her lips trembled. She reached out and tucked the wayward lock behind his ear. "There's nothing in this world I would rather do, Quinten Parker."

He took her lips to his and sealed their future.

It was a private affair, simple but elegant, with only Rae and Quinn's closest friends in attendance. Gail stood teary-eyed as Rae's maid of honor, and Nick had flown in from Europe to serve as best man, along with his wife Parris who sang a song she'd composed especially for the occasion.

And Rae had given Quinn the most selfless gift of all, allowing Remy to walk her down the aisle of the tiny Baptist Church.

Even Maxine flew in with Taylor, Jamel and her brand new daughter, Mia, in tow. And Maxine couldn't have been more proud or as moved as when Jamel handed his father the ring to place on Rae's finger. Taylor, always in tune to his wife's every emotion, wrapped his arm protectively around her shoulder, and pulled her close. "She'll be there for him now, Max," he whispered.

She sniffed and nodded. "I know." She hugged her daughter to her.

"Rae," Quinn began in an almost intimate whisper, nearly overcome by the simple beauty of his wife-to-be. "When you came into my life, I was a broken and empty man. Thinking about tomorrow was not a reality for me. Until you. You've made me whole, Rae—finally. You made me take my life back and learn how to live again and know that it is all right to love again, to love you with all my heart, all my soul, for as long as you'll have me. I won't leave you, I promise not to hurt you. I'll listen with my heart, I'll give you all of me, everyday of my life for as long as I live."

Unchecked tears streamed down Gail's face as she experienced up-close what it was like to be truly loved—adored.

Rae took the simple gold band from the satin pillow and placed it on Quinn's finger.

"With you in my life, I know now that anything is possible. We have come through the fire together, singed but whole. We have witnessed the hurts, the joys and triumphs in each other's lives and became better because of them. We have found the one thing that people spend their whole lives searching for—unquestionable, unshakable love. For you, Quinten

Parker, I will open my heart, my mind, my soul. I will let go of the past and move boldly into the future with you at my side. I promise to grow with you, share with you, love you with all my heart—for as long as time will allow."

Vera held a simple white handkerchief to her eyes to stem the tears of joy, though bittersweet. She was thankful that she was given this moment in Quinn's life, a memory that she could cling to.

Mrs. Finch patted Vera's shoulder as she watched with pride the boy she'd seen grow into a real man. A strong sense of pride filled her, knowing that in some small way she played a role. Her job was done. She'd come into his life at one of its lowest points, saw him through his marriage to Nikita and his loss of her. Saw him learn to become a father to Jamel. But what she'd nightly prayed for had finally come to pass, he'd met that one true person that was destined for him. Rae Lindsay was the woman his soul had been searching for all along.

". . . I now pronounce you husband and wife. Please . . . kiss your beautiful bride."

"With pleasure," Quinn murmured, slowly pulling Rae into his arms and capturing the subtle sweetness of her lips, loving her with all his heart for the whole world to see.

Epilogue

"Phoenix," the hit single composed by Parker and Parker, set a new standard for contemporary jazz, and both Quinn and Rae were in demand for interviews, club dates, and recording contracts.

But they took it in stride, simply enjoying their life together and coming to accept that their love was what made their life complete, not their music. It was only a small part of who they were.

Yes, Quinn was back in the studio from time to time, and Rae still composed, but mostly from home. She enjoyed her role as wife again and was determined to do it right this time. And that meant everything.

Quinn had just returned from checking on his mother, something he'd gotten into the habit of doing once a week. It was real hard at first, and a part of him resisted, while another part of him would push himself up the stairs and through her apartment door.

During the past year, they'd developed a relationship of sorts, tentatively giving over a part of themselves to the other. It would never be what it might have been, but it was a start at something.

"Honey, I'm home," Quinn called out jokingly.

Rae emerged at the top of the stairs, clothed in nothing but a near sheer teddy that revealed more than it covered. "Is that any way to greet your woman?" she asked in a taunting voice. She crooked her finger and beckoned him upstairs. And his welcome-home treat would keep him coming through that door night after night.

Cuddling in the afterglow of their loving, Rae weighed carefully what she was about to say.

"Quinn. You asleep?"

"Hmmm. Depends." He pulled her close.

"I need to talk to you about something."

His eyes sprung open, his senses on alert.

"I . . . was thinking that we should move out to the coast."

He was fully awake now. "The coast? Why? Our life is here."

"Well . . ." she said coyly. "I just figured it would be great if Jamel got to know his . . . new sister or brother . . . and that it would be wonderful if he could, we could all . . ."

"Rae?" His eyes sparkled with delight. "Rae?" he repeated.

She nodded, a smile streaking across her face.

He pulled her to him, kissed her deep and long,

trying to say to her without words just how much she meant to him, what she was willing to do for him, how eternally thankful he would be. Reluctantly he eased back and looked at her, really looked at her, searching for all the signs of the life that bloomed inside her—a part of him.

"And I was thinking that since we'll be giving up this place, that your mother could move in, keep Mrs. Finch company, and . . ."

She rambled on, and all he could do was laugh, knowing that this woman would be orchestrating his life for a very long time. And it was all good.

Dear Reader:

At long last Quinn has finally found not only happiness with Rae, but also answers to all the questions that have haunted him for years. I think Rae and Quinn will have the perfect life together—at least I hope so!

I want to thank you all for your untiring support over the years—the letters, the E-mails, and the smiling faces at book signings around the country. The twelve-year ride has been a wonderful one, and I will always cherish every minute of it.

I look forward to many more stories, toiling over the computer keys to get the scene "just right," hoping to entertain and hopefully enlighten you all with the magic of words. To get a look at my upcoming projects or to join my reading group, log on to my Web site at: http://www.donnahill1.com.

So . . . until next time,

Donna

For a look at one of
Donna Hill's previous books,
A PRIVATE AFFAIR,
just turn the page. . . .

Ain't No Mountain High

The spring weekend was far too short, Nikita mused, pulling her Benz into the parking garage where her new offices were housed. She handed her monthly coupon to the attendant.

Grant had definitely lived up to his pledge to take care of her. There wasn't a thing she'd asked for that he hadn't given or done.

The only thing that Grant was lacking was an ability to totally satisfy her. He wasn't an inconsiderate lover, just an unimaginative one. She had yet to feel the sparks of undeniable desire boil in her veins for Grant. Never had. But back then, that first time around, she hadn't known the difference. Until Quinn.

There was no denying that she and Quinn, physically, had fit like two pieces of a puzzle. She squirmed uncomfortably in her seat at the titillating thought.

It was the other aspects of their lives that stayed in turmoil.

But, now she had Grant. Grant was good for her. And she was finally beginning to accept having someone take care of things for her for a change. And it felt good.

She supposed.

Moving toward her office, she felt that old familiar rush surge through her veins when she looked at the gold lettering on the door. *Harrell Publishing, Inc.* Hers. Her hard work and determination had paid off.

Her heels clicked with purpose across the marble floors, the sound of a polished businesswoman who had the right contacts, the right clothes, a devoted staff, and the right man. That old Virginia Slims commercial ran in her head "You've come a long way, Baby."

Nikita opened the entrance door of the office and was thrown into open-mouthed shock, when a thundering round of "Welcome back!" nearly hurled her back out the way she'd come in.

For several breathless seconds, she just stood there, her hand pressed against her chest, willing her heart to be still, while her staff of ten enveloped her in hugs and kisses of welcome.

Her eyes stung and her throat felt tight. This was the last thing she'd expected.

"I . . . don't . . . know what to say." She sniffed back impending tears.

"Just tell everyone how much you missed them so we can dig into these bagels," a familiar voice rang out from the back of the group.

Nikita looked up and her eyes widened, then narrowed. She pointed an accusing finger in Grant's direction. "You . . . you knew all along. You sneak!"

"I confess." He made his way toward her. "But they swore me to secrecy," he said, kissing her on the cheek.

"I'll pay you back later, Bud," she said, low enough for only him to hear.

She looked around and beamed. "You guys are really something. This is great."

Monica slipped her arm around Nikita's waist. " 'Scuse us a minute, Grant." She squeezed between the couple, pulling Nikita aside. "Girl, it's good to have you back." She ushered her toward the spread of donuts, bagels, juice, and coffee. "Just want to warn you. I set up a lunch meeting with that new author I told you about. He'll be in town tomorrow, then we can talk contracts."

"No problem, as far as I know. I'd have rather had some more time to go over the manuscript before meeting with him. But I'll try to get through as much of it as possible between now and then."

"You would have thought, with a novel like this, he'd have gone to one of the major houses for the big bucks," Monica said, "but hey, don't look a gift horse in the mouth. Right?"

She was getting that funny feeling in her stomach again, as if she were on a roller coaster. She smiled faintly. "Right."

Grant stepped up to the duo. "Listen, Sweetheart, I have to get back to my office."

Just that quickly, she'd forgotten he was there. "Oh, Grant." She blinked. "How did you manage to get away? Those tightwad accountants are sticklers for time."

He grinned. "I told my boss I had an appointment with the IRS."

Monica gave him a blank look, obviously not getting the joke.

Grant's sense of humor somehow always reflected numbers or accounts in some form or fashion. It took some getting used to, and his years in the Air Force had only made him stiffer.

Nikita tiptoed and brushed her lips against his. "Thanks for coming, Sweetheart."

"Pick you up after work?"

"I drove in. I didn't feel like being at the mercy of a cabdriver today."

"Then I'll see you at six. Try to be ready."

"Very funny." That was the one bone of contention between her and Grant. He was a stickler for time, just like that group he worked with. Often it bordered on annoying. Her thoughts had already shifted to the manuscript, and she was actually eager for Grant to leave so she could get to work.

After the staff had devoured the morning feast and returned to their desks, Nikita and Monica retreated to Nikita's office.

"Wow, this feels good." Nikita sat, then leaned back against her high-back leather swivel chair, just like the one she'd seen in her little girl dreams.

She let out a breath. "Okay, so let's have it. What's the story on the new author?"

Monica sat down, a Cheshire cat grin on her butterscotch face, and crossed her long legs, purposely dragging out and dramatizing the moment. "We-l-l, as I mentioned in the fax, about three weeks ago I got this package—no agent, just regular mail. I started to just put it aside, but when I had some time on my hands I took a peek. Let's put it this way I started reading and couldn't stop. It's that good, Nikita. It's hot. It had me laughin', cryin', and swearin'. I've read few stories like that, written by a man, with so much passion and insight." She shook her head. "This author has talent to the bone."

"Can't wait to read it."

"I'll bring it right in." Monica popped up from her seat, went to the door, and stopped. "Hey, Niki, didn't someone named Quinn work at the magazine from time to time just before I started?"

Her stomach rose and fell. She focused on her appointment book while she answered. "Yes. Why?"

"Q. J. Parker. His name is Quinten. Wouldn't it be something if it was the same guy?" She hurried out.

Her world started to spin.

Moments later, Monica reappeared with the box containing the manuscript. "Here it is. Enjoy. I have a stack of stuff on my desk to take care of. See you later."

Nikita's eyes trailed to the box as if magnetically drawn. "Sure," she mumbled. "Thanks."

For several interminable moments, she just sat there staring at the covered box, teetering on the threshold of indecision. A part of her, the publisher part, was eager to read the contents. But the woman, the one who was still trying to put her life back together, hesitated. Hesitated, because if Quinn had written a book that took the reader's breath away, she didn't know if she would be woman enough to publish it. No matter what the rewards.

She turned her attention to her calendar, checking

production dates for upcoming titles and reacquainting herself with appointments that had been made months ago.

She spent the next three hours returning phone calls, reviewing bills, and catching up on correspondence. But her gaze and her thoughts kept drifting back and forth to the box.

"This is ridiculous." She swallowed and tossed her pen down on her desk. She reached for the cover and snatched it open.

There, staring at her in big bold letters was *A Private Affair,* by Q. J. Parker. She inhaled a shaky breath and reached for the first page when the phone rang, a momentary reprieve.

"Imani. How are you?"

"Not so good, Ms. Harrell. My contract says that I have no input about the cover art. That's totally unfair. Suppose the art work is horrid?"

Generally, Nikita didn't take these calls. She let Monica handle them. But Imani Angoza was a brilliant, budding novelist who needed to be handled with kid gloves. Although she loved Monica to pieces, Monica had a way of expressing her displeasure that wasn't always too subtle.

"You did sign the contract. And I know you had your attorney look it over, because she returned it to me personally before I went away."

"But Ms. Harrell. I—"

"Tell you what, when the cover layouts are submitted I'll call you and we'll review them together. How does that sound?"

"Great. Thank you, Ms. Harrell," she said, finally losing the whine in her voice. "I don't mean to be a nag, but this is important to me."

"Of course it is. It's important to me, also. I'll keep you up to date on the progress."

"Thank you. I'll call you. Soon."

Nikita smiled. *I know you will.* "Do that."

She leaned back in her seat, resting her head against the cool leather. She closed her eyes. Her head was starting to pound, and when she opened her eyes and looked up at the antique grandfather clock that sat in the corner of her office, it was past one.

Well, she'd successfully gotten through her morning without reading one word of the manuscript. She sighed. She'd planned to cut her day short anyway, in preparation for the evening. If she left now, she'd have plenty of time to take care of her running around, read some of the contents of the box, and be ready in time for Grant to pick her up at six.

She shut off her computer, packed her briefcase, and tucked the box under her arm. The office had cleared out for lunch by the time she came out front. She left a note on Monica's desk.

Impatiently, she shifted from one foot to the other, waiting for the elevator. Grant was such a pain about time, and could make her entire evening an exercise in misery if she weren't ready. She didn't want anything to ruin her reunion with Parris.

They'd made plans to meet after her show for a late dinner. Just the two of them. To catch up.

While she waited impatiently at a red light, she checked her watch. Time seemed to be moving at an incredible speed today. Then, when she looked up at the street signs, she realized that she'd taken the wrong route home and had completely bypassed the cleaners. She had to pick up the dress she'd planned to wear tonight and stop at the market, which was in the opposite direction. She took a left at the intersection and sped off.

What's wrong with me? Can't seem to stay focused. Maybe it's just the after-effects of the trip.

She stopped by the market and selected the few items that she needed to prepare a light meal for her and Grant.

Jumping back into the Benz, she pulled out into traffic and zipped around a slow moving Caddy.

As much as she didn't want to admit it, she knew it was the resurgence of old thoughts and feelings about Quinn that was playing havoc with her emotions.

Annoyed with herself—her weakness and inability to seal her heart against memories of Quinn—she slapped away the lock with the little seashell, the one that now reached below her shoulders, and turned on two wheels onto her block.

She was almost grateful that Grant would be coming in a few hours. If anyone could put order back in her life, Grant could.

Nikita hung the dress in the closet, chuckling on her way to the kitchen. She knew Parris would leap at the chance to steal it from her if she wasn't careful.

"Not this time, Sistah." That dress had been pure extravagance. She'd paid nearly a month's rent for the creation.

She began gathering the ingredients for an early meal with Grant. She whipped together a pasta salad on a bed of fresh spinach, lightly seasoned with oil, just the way Grant liked it.

Yet, no matter how hard she tried, memories, visions, and desires for Quinn seemed to taunt her, come to life with every blink of her eye.

Her hands had the slightest tremor as she replaced the condiments. Her heart beat a little faster when she briefly shut her eyes and imagined his scent. The assault on her senses was almost more than she could stand. What was worse was accepting how desperately she still missed him.

"Go away!" She pounded her fist against the yellow countertop that they'd prepared so many meals on together, and lowered her head. "Go away," she whispered.

Totally frazzled, she returned to the living room, the box with the manuscript calling out to her from the coffee table where she'd left it. She moved slowly toward it, picking up its weight and settling herself down on the couch.

She pulled off the box top and the cover page beneath and began to read. . . .

Steam rolled off the New York City streets in waves, pushing intrepid strollers to seek refuge in the cool confines of cafes, malls, and local bars. The heat this summer afternoon was beyond intense. But that wasn't why the folks on Malcolm X Boulevard and 135th Street would remember that day. No, it wouldn't be remembered for the heat, but for the many lives that were irrevocably changed by an ugly twist of fate.

The small church was packed. Neighbors and friends stood shoulder to shoulder, whispering among themselves how tragic it all was. Marcus stood alone—from the world and with his grief. He couldn't count how many times he'd asked himself: why his sister?

Parts of him felt as if they'd break into a million pieces.

Other parts of him were infused with an anger that was barely contained. The pain was so deep, so pervasive, that it stooped his proud shoulders.

He tried to pay attention to what the minister was saying. It was all a haze. The trip to Tracy's final resting place was a dream scene. Words of condolence were met with his vacant stare and empty smiles. The sultry, steamy days that followed blended together into a nothingness.

Marcus forced himself to go out every day, to the street that was his home. He seemed driven by forces that he could not control. He pushed himself with a vengeance. Maybe if he had worked harder, faster, none of this would have happened. He and Tracy would have been out of the clutches of the drive-bys, the drugs, the gangs. It was his fault. And he felt so alone—until he met her.

He'd been sitting in the local jazz club, nursing a glass of Jack Daniels, when she'd walked into the club. He felt his heart pick up just a notch, and the hair on the back of his neck began to tingle with awareness. Even the music seemed to pulse with a little more intensity, like a scene in a movie building toward the climax.

He tossed down the last of his drink and watched her move—in what seemed like slow motion—across the crowded room. She wore a white, spaghetti strap T-shirt that molded to the curves of her breasts from the dampness that clung to her body like a satisfied lover.

She was a bit on the short side, Marcus noted, but she was packaged well. The pale-colored shorts cupped her round bottom in a most appealing way. Her curved legs were a glistening bare brown, the color of honey, her tiny feet encased in white deck shoes.

Marcus swallowed hard, and swore that the air-conditioning must have burst a circuit, because it was suddenly damned hot.

She signaled for the waiter and ordered a Pepsi with lemon.

He slid slowly around on the bar stool until he had a view diagonally across from where she sat, apparently very content with her surroundings. She wasn't meeting anyone.

He didn't know how he knew it. He just did.

She seemed to sense his approach. Slowly, she raised her eyes. They didn't register alarm, Marcus realized, but acceptance. He watched her swallow the last of her drink, and followed the path of the cool liquid down the line of her slender throat. She smiled when he stopped and stood above her.

"I've been watching you for a while," Marcus said. He'd memorized the perfect slope of her brown eyes, the arch of her chiseled cheekbones, the curve of her full lips, but up close they were even more intense. The sensation had him reeling.

He took a quick breath and slid into the seat next to her. "I'm glad you're alone." He looked casually around the darkened room. "You aren't waiting for anyone," he stated more than asked.

"What makes you think that?"

Her voice was low and throaty, inviting, just like he'd imagined it would be.

"Because we've been waiting to meet each other for a long time. The time is now." He gave her a slow, lazy smile. "My name is Marcus Collins, and yours . . ." He reached across the table and took her hand. He felt her tremble, and instantly knew that she wasn't as full of all the bravado she'd displayed. That tiny realization inched open the doorway to emotions that he'd nailed shut.

And he was suddenly afraid. Afraid of what feeling again would do to him.

Through a veil of tears, she wiped her eyes and continued to read, reliving their life together, page after page, the loving, the laugher, the fighting, and his secret pain.

. . . He wasn't sure anymore where he began and she ended. The more he gave, the more she wanted, never seeing that all he wanted, all he needed in his life, was for her to love him, just to be loved for who he was; a simple man. Maybe not the perfect man, but one who was willing to try, who was doing all that he could, in his own way, to make her happy. Even, it seemed, to give up a part of himself in the process.

That Christmas, at her parents' house, was the beginning of the end. He didn't realize it then, but it was.

In vivid, anguished clarity the eloquent prose painted a portrait of a man emasculated, humiliated, in front of the woman who claimed to love him. Why, the writer asked, would she have put him in that position when she said she cared? So he'd put on his front, his don't-give-a-damn attitude, hidden behind his facade of indifference, and she hadn't seemed to notice.

But it wasn't her fault. He couldn't blame her. Never would. It was all she knew. She came from a world where everything went according to plan. There was no struggle, no hard-core reality check. She stayed so busy planning the future, she couldn't see the now. But still he tried, until he couldn't try anymore.

And how could he tell her what was going on inside? He'd never really learned to share emotions. That was for women, he believed. She saw him as a tower of strength. No weakness. This vision of invincibility. He couldn't show any other face to her. Not now. Not after all this time. The only way he knew how to show her that he cared was by giving her what she needed. And giving her his body. It was the only time he could let go, bridge the gap that separated them. There was no other plateau on which he could reach her expectations. It was only there that he filled her.

And finally, even for him, it was no longer enough.

She didn't want to read any more. Didn't want to feel those feelings again. She'd never known. Never understood how deep his feelings went. How empty he felt without his sister, how guilty he felt about his mother's abandonment, the loss of the women in his life, his fear that it would only happen again. She'd tried to fill it by making him do, do more, do better.

And then it hit her like a surprise left hook. She'd done to Quinn exactly what her parents had done to her. And just as it had pushed her away, it pushed him away, too. He had to find his own way.

And he had.

"Oh, God, Quinn, I'm so sorry. So sorry."

She covered her face with her hands and wept.

* * *

On the ride to the club she tried to keep up a cheerful front, to smile in all the right places, say the right thing. But it took all she had not to come apart.

Grant looked at her after another bout of silence. "You want to tell me what's wrong, Nikita?"

She forced another smile. "Nothing. Just tired, I guess, and anxious to see Parris again."

"You sure? You seem totally preoccupied—"

"I'm fine, Grant really. Just . . . please . . . leave it alone."

"I would if I knew what it was I was leaving alone." He focused all of his attention on driving, hoping that she'd finally tell him about whatever was bothering her.

The club was packed by the time she and Grant arrived. Michelle, still the hostess, wiggled around the patrons and showed them to their tables. Jewel and her soul mate Taj were already seated.

Taj stood and kissed her cheek. "Hey, Lady. Long time."

"Listen to you, Mr. World Traveler." She turned toward Grant and introduced him to Taj.

They ordered drinks. Nikita stuck to her usual, but within the next few minutes she wished she'd gotten something stronger.

"Good evening, everyone," Nick said, stepping up to the mike. "Tonight we have a special treat for you. Not only will my lovely wife, the incomparable Parris McKay, be singing for you, but we have a special guest—a former member of the band who will play some selections from his soon to be released CD . . . Mr. Quinten Parker. Give it up!"

Her heart slammed in her chest, arresting her breathing. Her head pounded.

The audience roared its approval.

Quinn rose from a seat at a table on the far side of the room, moving toward the stage in the slow, easy gait that she'd memorized, taking his place behind the black and whites, in the single spotlight that captured him.

She froze. Seeing him again . . . here, now, in the place where it really all began, pushed away all the time that was lost, the hurt that was experienced. And time suddenly stood still as he took them on a musical odyssey, his fingers caressing the keys the way they'd once played along her spine.

Grant had his arm around her shoulder and felt her stiffen, then begin to tremble, ever so slightly.

He whispered in her ear, "We can leave if you want."

She looked at him, really looked at him, and realized that he understood. Probably always had, without her ever saying a word. And he'd been by her side . . . anyway. The way Maxine had always been for Quinn.

She smiled and squeezed his hand. "No. I need to stay."

He nodded, kissed her temple, and turned his gaze back to the stage.

The club had emptied out. The strains of music from the jukebox filtered through the spaces. Everyone was gone and, to her surprise, it was Grant who'd insisted that she stay behind and "work it out." He'd given her a soft look of understanding and perhaps regret. "I'll be home if you need me," he'd said.

Nikita picked up her glass and then put it back down, looking across at Parris. "When did you know he was coming?"

"About an hour before I went on." She looked at her friend. "Are you okay?"

"I will be. Finally, I think I will be." She took in a long breath and let it go. "I know everything now, Parris. Everything that went wrong and what went right," she said in a faraway voice.

"What do you mean, Hon?"

She looked into Parris's green eyes. "He wrote a novel. Yes. Quinten Parker wrote a novel." She turned away for a moment. "About us. Our life together." She slowly shook her head. "I saw myself through his eyes, Parris. I was never able to see that before. Maybe I didn't want to."

"And?"

"He did the best he could. Loved me in his own way. We didn't give each other a real chance." Her throat tightened. She looked up and saw him walking across the floor, toward their table.

Parris got up, touched his arm as she walked past him, and disappeared into the back room.

His smile was soft, hesitant, but those damned dimples were still there, and she smiled.

"Still drinking that lemon Pepsi."

That old familiar voice surrounded her, worked its way down to her bones.

He reached out his hand to take hers, as the jukebox pumped out Chaka Khan's "Your Love is All I Know."

She stepped into his embrace, as if she'd never left.

And they moved easily to the music, finding their own special rhythm, the poignant words touching them in their own way.

"I had to come back. To see you, Niki. Tell you I was sorry," he said in a ragged voice, hugging the familiar body close to his.

"I know," she whispered. "I know." She took a breath, stepped back, and looked up into his eyes. "I read the book, Quinn. Most of it—"

"I needed you to . . . I found a way, Niki . . . just like you always said I would. I . . . tried to use what I'd always had, to say what I've never said to you. . . . It wasn't your fault, Baby. Never was. And I can't keep runnin' away anymore. Runnin' to the familiar, takin' the easy way out, where it's safe. You never gave me no easy way, Niki, and it scared me."

She struggled for air.

"I'm not scared anymore."

"Where do I go . . . after all that we've been through . . ." Chaka cried.

Nikita swallowed back the lump in her throat, her eyes sparkling with the tears she'd sworn she'd never shed again.

And then he said the words he'd never uttered to another soul. "I love you, Nikita, from the depths of my soul . . . I know that now . . . maybe I always did."

Her world seemed to spin and she barely breathed. How long had she waited to hear him say he loved her? Those precious words. She inhaled deeply, and stepped out of his embrace. She reached up and stroked his cheek, pushing aside a stray lock of his hair.

She stood on tiptoes, touched her mouth to his, to

those all too familiar lips, lingering a moment, just . . . long enough.

"You know how to find me, when you're ready."

She turned, picked her purse up from the table, and walked out, knowing that her tomorrow, her forever, was now finally hers.

Quinn watched her go, his soul finally at peace, crossed the room to the bar, and ordered a glass of Jack Daniels.

Nikita never made things easy. She was his light, always had been. He'd just been too blind to see it.

He smiled.

Here All the Time

She'd made up her mind that if he didn't come back she'd be all right. She'd press on. But damnit, the past thirty-six hours had been the longest "I don't care" hours of her natural born life.

Work was one salvation. And she'd just about burnt herself out at the gym, hoping that she'd be so exhausted she'd just collapse into bed.

Nothing happening.

She didn't know folks could stay awake for damn near two days without going into a coma or something.

One more night. Just one, and she'd know for sure. One way or the other.

She locked up the office and walked the half-block to where her five-year-old Honda Accord was parked. Got a good deal on it and it ran like a dream. She stuck the key in the lock, thinking about her long night ahead. "Don't play with me, Q. Just don't even try it."

Taking the long route home, she stopped at some of the antique shops, just to look, then decided to pick up some fresh vegetables and a bottle of wine.

Everything else failed at putting her to sleep. Since she wasn't a wine drinker, maybe it would do the trick.

By the time she reached her neat little home, it had grown dark. And she felt the loneliness settle over her just like the clouds hanging up over the rooftops. Nights were the hardest. Always had been.

She opened the door, picked up the mail and flipped on all the lights as she went—saying "hey" to all her plants—needing the light, but needing more than that somebody to come home to, especially tonight.

He stood watching her from the top of the stairs as she fussed over her plants, cussed at the bills in her hand, in all her earthy beauty. And it made him smile, inside and out.

"Hey, Girl."

She shut her eyes and breathed in and out real slow, wanting to make sure it wasn't the lack of sleep playing tricks on her.

Okay, she had herself together.

She turned around, slowly, because if it was her imagination she wanted it to last just a minute longer.

She looked up. It wasn't a dream. It wasn't a trick.

She tipped her head to the side and put her hand on her hip. "You here to stay, Q?"

He started down the stairs. He watched those perfect little breasts of hers rise and fall beneath her yellow silk blouse. *Only Max could wear yellow silk.*

He stood in front of her, looking down into those eyes that challenged him to answer her . . . with his heart . . . with the truth.

"I think you know, Max. You always have," he whispered.

And her eyes filled and tears ran down her cheeks even though she'd promised herself she wouldn't cry, one way or another. *Didn't make sense to let a man know he had you like that. But . . . what the hell.*

He pulled her into his arms, tight, feeling her all around him, in his heart, deep in his soul. Right there all the time. His friend . . . all that she ever could be.

She tilted her head back, smiling through her tears, that little toothpick gap winking at him.

"I know," she breathed. "I know."

And she knew she'd be okay.

ABOUT THE AUTHOR

Donna Hill was first published in 1987 with the short story "The Long Walk." Since that time she has added twenty-one titles to her credit, including six novellas and fifteen published novels. She has two more single titles and two novellas scheduled for release this year. She has been featured in *Essence*, the *Daily News*, *USA Today*, *Today's Black Woman*, and *Black Enterprise*, among many others, and has appeared on numerous radio and television programs across the country. Her work has appeared on the Emerge, Ingram Books, and Blackboard best-sellers lists, and three of her novels have been adapted for television. She is the recipient of the 1998 Romantic Times Career Achievement Award and the Vivian Stephens Career Achievement Award Nominee for 2000. Donna works full time as a Public Relations Associate for the Queens Borough Public Library system, and organizes author-centered events and workshops through her promotions and management company. She lives with her family in Brooklyn, NY. You can visit her Web site at http://www.donnahill1.com.